Scríobh
Scribbles

VOLUME I

Scríobh: Carrigallen Creative Writing Group

Copyright © 2016

Scríobh: Carrigallen Creative Writing Group

Typeset 12pt Times New Roman

Book Cover & Design by Julie Williams

Compiled by Kevin Patrick

All rights reserved.

ISBN:10:153519555X
ISBN-13:978-1535195553

To Friendship:

SCRÍOBH: CARRIGALLEN CREATIVE WRITING GROUP

past, present and future.

CONTENTS

	Introduction & Acknowledgements	VIII
1	The Final	**1**
2	The Hidden Princess: A Fairy Tale	**6**
3	Brave Men	**11**
4	New Beginnings	**13**
5	Veritas?	**20**
6	The Hellfire Club	**21**
7	The Lost Night	**31**
8	The Troll's Tooth	**34**
9	His World	**39**
10	The Phone Call	**47**
11	Merging Traffic	**50**
12	True Empathy	**61**
13	The Late Lamented	**63**
14	A Jar of Pickled Onions	**66**
15	St. Joseph's Man	**69**

16	Window	**73**
17	Two Soldiers	**78**
18	Behind Bars	**83**
19	A Stolen Day	**91**
20	A Small Leak Will Sink a Big Ship	**95**
21	Coffee & Insomnia	**99**
22	Revenge	**100**
23	Death Notices	**111**
24	The Final Solution	**113**
25	Goodbye	**119**
26	The Dance Off	**121**
27	Famous Seamus	**126**
28	Snow Angels	**128**
29	Variations On a Morning	**132**
	The Authors	**134**
	Writing In The Round	**142**

INTRODUCTION

Carrigallen Creative Writing Group began in March 2011 when local librarian, Helen Corcoran, approached Susie Minto, a trained creative writing group leader, with a view to setting up a writing group. Under initial funding from Leitrim Arts Office and Leitrim Libraries the group met in Carrigallen Library and soon established itself.

After Susie left to pursue other work abroad, in spring 2014, the core members of the group agreed to continue and rebrand as Scríobh: Carrigallen Creative Writing Group, on a self-run basis, seeking to progress further in the craft of writing.

Our members are adults from Leitrim, Cavan, Longford and beyond who all share a passion for creative writing in stories, poems, fan fiction, prose poems and reflective pieces. Using the trigger system under the Amherst Writers and Artists method, the group progressed to structured critiques of work and benefitted from guest facilitators such as poet Monica Corish and writer Maggie Barnard, to develop their writing skills further.

Indeed many of the members have now seen their work published, locally and nationally, and several have been the recipients of awards and gained local recognition, which has increased confidence and belief for all. So much so, that we arrived at the point where an idea first floated by the shores of the Town Lake in Carrigallen two years ago, that we should publish a book or collection of our writings, is now laid before you.

This collection is offered in the spirit of being a tentative punt onto the open water of publishing and is comprised of 'polished pieces', that is, writing that has in many cases originated from a creative writing session and has been polished up by the writer at home, then brought back to be read out loud by the author and constructively critiqued by the rest of the group. This level of trust is not easily reached nor is the confidence to read aloud your own writing, even semi-publicly. It requires a courage which we hope you will recognise and value in this initial collection.

Thanks in large amounts are due to Leitrim Libraries for the use of Carrigallen Library for our meetings, along with host and founder member, Helen Corcoran. Also to Mary Kiernan a member of the Carrigallen Readers Group, for her excellent proofing, which substantially improved the clarity of the text, and to Harry Browne of Dublin Writing Group 'InkSplinters' for providing invaluable tips to help us navigate our virgin voyage in publishing.

September 2016.

SCRÍOBH: CARRIGALLEN CREATIVE WRITING GROUP

THE FINAL

Lionel Mullally

Kevin Sherry could feel his blood boil. He was sure he could. Either that or it was the start of a heart attack and he hoped that at forty-six years of age he was still too young for that. But, you never know. And this shower of players weren't doing the blood pressure any good. Chatting and talking in the dressing room only minutes from the start of a county final.

And against THEM!! The neighbouring parish! And this lot were chatting.

He roared them into silence.

"Sweet mother of..." and stopped. He closed his eyes and breathed deep. This too shall pass, isn't that what his mother used to tell him.

He opened his eyes and looked around. At least they were quiet now.

"Right," he continued, "Regardless of what others may have said, this is not just another match. You cannot treat it as just another match. It's a final. And more importantly, it's against THEM!"

He pointed at the wall and beyond as he roared that last word.

He let it sink in.

"I won't even mention their name in this room. That shower thinks they have it already won; that it's just a case of showing up here and claiming the cup. You've to stop them and teach them a lesson. Some of you are related to some of them, I know that. Ignore that. You'll still be cousins later when it's over. But, as of right now, focus. This is the final. If they win, they'll be driving around our town tonight blowing the horns of the cars on their victory parade and yelling out the windows at you lot as you stand there and have to take it. If they win that's what's ahead of you!"

He paused for effect. He'd practiced this speech in front of the bathroom mirror until he was happy with it. Timing and passion were essential. Like the game itself he believed.

"I want you to give it all out there. Leave it all on the pitch. We'll bring the subs on and off to make maximum impact. But you have to go that extra inch. Reach out...stretch...keep going for that one inch more and when you put them all together it'll be enough to get you over the line. I want our keeper bored in this match because you lot" he pointed at the defenders "won't let them past that thirteen metre line on the pitch. Understood?"

There were a few nods of heads.

He roared – "Understood?"

The heads shot up and a resounding "YES" assaulted him.

"Midfield, no messing or fannying about. Attack constantly. Get that ball into the forwards. Defend when you have to. Keep tracking back. Hassle them, get in their faces and break their hearts. Don't give them any room. OK?"

A loud "Yes."

"Forwards, your job is the easiest one. You score."

They laughed. He let them.

"You score and keep that scoreboard moving. Remember no fancy..." he hesitated, "stuff. Remember KISS. Keep it simple..." they joined in with "STU-PID!!"

"And, at the end, Captain; where are you? There you are. At the end give them the token three cheers. You better have your speech ready."

"Now, are you all clear? You've done this a thousand times before at training. You keep the ball. If they get it, you fight for it back. If I don't see you fighting for it you're coming off! Do I make myself clear? You fight for and win every ball. Forwards; that goes for you too. Win those kick outs. Hassle their defenders. Scare them into mistakes."

Laughing could be heard through the wall from the dressing room down the hall.

He went quiet.

"Do you hear that?" he whispered as violently as he could.

"They're laughing. Laughing! They're enjoying this. They're celebrating already before a ball has been kicked. They're laughing at us! At you!"

He said nothing as they heard the laughter diminish.

"So let's do something about this. About them. Fight for every ball. Win every ball or make them regret tackling you and make them afraid to do it again. If you can't go round them, go through them. They'll get the hint then. Punish them and let them know they're in a fight, a real game. Don't let them drive around our town tonight with the cup. Do I make myself clear?"

"Yes"

"Louder"

"Yes!"

"Louder. Let them hear ya!"

"YES!!"

The blood was up. He ordered them to stand, to put in their gum shields. He walked along the line as he spoke, smiling, nodding, patting the shoulders.

"Captain, you'll lead them out. Put on your game faces. Decide you're winning this final here and now. And then, you'll be the first. The first county champions in this jersey. The first from this town of ours. And that cannot and never will be taken from you. You're here on merit. Go out and show them why. Win!! Be the first. The first under 12 Ladies county champions this town has ever had. Now, out with ya!!"

A small hand shot up.

"I forgot my bobbin."

He removed a spare from his wrist and handed it over and she deftly put the pony tail in place.

"Have you all got enough clips?"

They nodded yes as they lined up, chattering again and started to run out as he opened the door.

Out they went, as determined as only ten and eleven year olds can be.

… SCRÍOBH: CARRIGALLEN CREATIVE WRITING GROUP

THE HIDDEN PRINCESS: A FAIRYTALE

Aisling Doonan

There once lived a young maiden, a hidden princess. She lived in a small cottage with warm pink bricks and sandstone quoins that glowed as they soaked up the sun and held the light still. White sashed windows pointed skyward like candle flames, raising your eyes to the steeply gabled roof and delicate gingerbread trim. Inside was dim, with dust settling in the corners, swirling gently in the currents as she paced from room to room. The walls were dark and cracked, the ceilings low, awkward angles meeting sharply in the claustrophobic spaces that held her captive.

The house nestled neatly next to a small wood, where the trees whispered their secrets to her and hummed gently in the breeze. She loved to walk there, to listen to the chorus of birds and their musical chatter. She walked to remind herself that life was beautiful. She used every colour and sound to soothe the anxious fluttering that began in her chest as soon as she awoke. Though she looked serene and content, her smile hid the raging squall that threatened to drown her. A constant barrage of thoughts assaulted her from every angle, the maelstrom so tangled she could not make sense or unravel it alone. So she walked and she sang, watching the speckled light dance on the silver birch that lined the avenue. The bleached wood was becoming honeyed as the light took on a deeper, vibrant wash in the early evening. Her surroundings bathed in a glow from an unearthly source.

She could travel no further than the end of the trees, her feet would not permit her to move beyond a certain point. They became leaden and clumsy and she struggled to move one foot in front of the other before they began to ache and pulse uncomfortably. As she struggled forward the discomfort gave way to pain which expanded in intensity till the torment grew too big for her to endure. So, she would return to the house in defeat, a little smaller than the day before. Each failure bound her tighter, keeping her low and covering her light.

One autumn, as the leaves began to crackle in anticipation, she lingered on the avenue. Her chest felt tight, the centre of her back prickled and her limbs were restless. She had reached the point where the misery and distress of her proximity to the end of her endurance threatened to crush her. Yet still she hesitated.

A disturbance in the air caught her attention and she raised her eyes to see a figure walking towards her. A man appeared from the road that led to the village. She held steady as he approached her, he was familiar yet unknown all at once. He greeted her pleasantly, held her eyes and smiled. She nodded and smiled in return as he passed her by, giving a small backward glance, before disappearing from view.

Autumn turned to winter, the leaves all blown to the earth, gathering in corners and melting into a soft wet mush. She continued to walk the avenue, a little further each day to greet her new friend.

"What is your name?"

"Freya" she replied, eyes locked to his to read from him.

They strolled down the avenue together, heads bent, deep in both thought and conversation. Lucas brought her a posy of pansies; Freya wove them through her hair happily and sketched him as he sat on an uprooted tree trunk. Content, they spent their days together lightly, always parting before the sun set. They would laugh and play, taking turns to tell stories and share secrets. They gently grew acquainted with each other as the days lengthened, taking pleasure in doing small kindnesses for each other.

"Let's walk towards the village." Lucas eagerly took Freya's hand and pulled her towards the end of the avenue but stopped when he met stubborn resistance.

"I can't leave here" she whispered standing firmly "It hurts too much."

"I don't understand" he frowned, "come with me, it's ok" he earnestly tugged her arm, but still met refusal.

"I have to stay, I can't leave" Freya withdrew her hand and slowly turned her back to him; she walked with her heavy burden back to the house and closed the door. Lucas left alone with a determination to unravel her defiance.

When spring finally arrived, the snow drifts revealed daffodils on every bank and green space; little buds appeared on the trees, the Birch being the first to erupt into new life. Birdsong was a constant soundtrack and Freya was feeling new and fresh and alive with it.

Lucas met her at the end of the avenue each day as usual and took her hand again to lead her towards the road.

"No!" Freya pulled back both in pain and disbelief at his insistence. "I told you, I can't."

Expecting her response Lucas replied "No, it's not that you can't, it's that you won't."

He took her hand firmly in his and drew her towards the road, his eyes holding her tight. Dazed she followed and the pain she felt began to shimmer and move within her chest. Still, he held her and moved slowly. She followed his lead and the agony loosened a little, the discomfort faded with each step, smiling she began to twirl. Radiance began to emanate from her body, a soft glow, growing brighter. Lucas caught a wisp of illumination that fell at her waist and tugged it as she moved in her little circle, her skirts flew out with her pirouette and the light rolled off her like a ribbon. He kept drawing the streamer to him as she spun, laughing happily with each turn. The torment that had lived within her had dissipated on contact with the brightness and she was aglow with relief. When his arms were laden with iridescent bindings Freya stopped turning. Her eyes were brilliant, her cheeks crimson and behind her back fluttering proudly were two glistening delicate wings, gossamer mesh, patterned with pearl lustre swirls. Freya was speechless at her transformation; she flexed her wings momentarily and enjoyed the euphoria.

"You did it, you broke the spell" she exclaimed "I'm free." Lucas shook her hand formally, warm and firm, but light enough to make her want to hold on tighter.

"You always were, you just didn't realise it" Lucas grinned, "Now put those wings away before someone sees them," he winked conspiratorially and stuffed her light into his jacket pocket with his own to keep safe.

BRAVE MEN

Helen Corcoran

As the dawn was breaking in the east, the cold May fog clung to their sparsely clad bodies as they stood, shoulder to shoulder, in front of the stone wall. All gallant, all scared but all were prepared to die for what they had fought for, Irish Independence. To die for their country which they loved dearly, to bring about freedom for all and to obtain a sovereign independent state was their ultimate goal.

Standing in darkness, wounded by centuries of struggle and determined to reverse the humiliations of Ireland's turbulent history, they listened for the commanding officers commands. Scared, not of dying, as all were prepared to make personal sacrifices, but that their deaths may be in vain after the guns fell silent? Scared for their loved ones, who would be left behind, to face life without them in an uncertain state?

They waited. They listened.

Only silence.

"What is happening?"

"Where are the commands?"

The commands which they had heard being shouted out for the past week, followed by the shrill of gunfire and then a thud, as another of their brave comrades fell to the ground, dead.

It was dark behind the blindfolds and the handcuffs were digging into their wrists. They waited, standing tall.

Silence.

In the distance, the clank of the heavy doors creaked open and footsteps approached in a marching order. They were really scared now. Their thoughts, 'Will we have failed or will we have struck the first blows for freedom?'

They prayed, and in unison shouted their last words "For Ireland!" as gun fire erupted.

Darkness.

Was it all in vain?

NEW BEGINNINGS

Ada Vance

Susan held the squat blue envelope to her lips. Turning it over in her hand she remembered another envelope, the same Basildon Bond Blue and matching note paper. Remembering the struggle she had then to get that letter just right, she paused and considered her decision, hesitated just a moment longer, then sealed the envelope.

She had chosen the day of the week carefully; today Sunday was the first day of the week and selected deliberately in the hope that it would be a good omen for the start of new beginnings.

On the bed lay the neatly packed old suitcase that had been an expensive purchase fifteen years ago when she went off to boarding school. It still looked good, of course it had had little use, back and forward to the convent for the summer, Christmas and Halloween breaks and stored away in-between. Some fragile keepsakes were lovingly wrapped in tissue paper and the diaries she had scribbled in almost every day for twelve years lay on the bottom.

It was amazing how the scribbling she did every evening had given a focus to her day. Mum had encouraged her and they both enjoyed this little end of day ritual. Tiny details about visitors, the weather, as well as important things like the day the solicitors came and the day she wrote to the nuns. Amazing how comforting the twelve years of journaling had been lately.

She opened the zip pouch inside the lining. There was her secret stash, cleverly creamed off over the years from the housekeeping budget and the takings from the pub. "Small amounts Susan," her mother had advised: - and exchange the small notes for bigger ones when you do the lodgements. She thought now that this defiance and cunning in her mother's character was a kind of rebellion against the affliction that she endured, and a way of compensating Susan. "Everyone needs insurance of some kind or other," she often said.

Carefully she straightened the wad of crisp notes and tucked them into her new Kipling travel bag. Sitting down on the edge of the bed she let her mind wander back over her teenage years and her dull early adulthood, "the best years of your life" people said, in Susan's case this was a joke.

Susan was an only girl with one older brother. She was a clever bright girl with a sunny nature and was considered to be the brains of the family. She had high hopes of becoming something worthwhile, her mind always whirled when she tried to pin down exactly what, but she was sure she would spend her days dressed in elegant fashionable outfits and good quality high shoes and boots with accessories that stood out and spoke volumes about her. There would be no quilted housecoat or comfortable grubby slippers. No cigarette stained ragged nails or dull hairstyle. She had plans. Teaching, or the bank, the nuns suggested, never mentioning the expense. Of course they knew there was money to fund such an ambitious plan. Her father owned a pub and a farm.

Then there was a blip and Susan's plans came to a halt.

Susan had studied hard for three years and she hugged herself with delight when the results rewarded her with top marks in the Junior Certificate, she was set for the next two years study and then the sky was the limit.

That year the summer holidays crept by slowly and at last it was time for back to boarding school. No more helping in the pub, cooking for the family and for the men who helped on the farm.

Several times she mentioned shopping for books, new school skirt and a present for her friend, Jenny's birthday was on September the 3rd, the day school opened and Jenny's mum would send something home-baked for tea on their first day back. The little party helped them settle back on a happy note. She shivered remembering the shock when her father dropped the bombshell.

"You are not going back this term, your mammy is sick, I want you to mind her and help with the work she does on the farm and in the bar. No nonsense now. We have to let the school know so good girl now, write a letter to the principal and say you are staying to mind Mammy for this year."

Angry and bewildered she wrote on the blue lined Basildon Bond paper. 'Dear Reverend Mother,' it began, 'I will not be coming back to school this term because my mammy is sick."

"What will I put now?" she asked him after the first paragraph,

"Tell them the truth, they'll know all about it" he said.

Often mentioned in whispers but never spoken out loud there was a name for the 'sickness' that plagued her mother, but Susan struggled with the spelling, it would need to be exactly right. She had seen it written, so to be sure, Susan walked slowly into the bar, reached for a bottle of Harp Lager, carried it to the sitting-room and carefully copied the word ALCOHOLIC. 'My mother is an alcoholic, I have to stay to help for a while and when she is better I can come back.'

Mam hadn't got better and the following year her brother had emigrated after a blazing row with their father. Susan wanted desperately to continue her education but the pressure was huge and all suggestions to employ someone full time, a companion-housekeeper or a manager for the business were dismissed.

Finally the ultimate carrot was dangled and Susan reluctantly resigned herself to grasp it. She would get the lot, the farm and the pub and the family home. Straight away the Will was drawn up and signed and sealed and life continued in much the same way as always until six months ago when her father died suddenly. The homilies at the funeral had said such nice things about him, upright pillar of the community, family man, supported every fundraising event.

The newly erected and highly polished gravestone stood proud and straight alongside dozens of other forgotten lichen covered specimens, some lying at drunken angles, their inscriptions dulled and hard to read.

Mam had died six weeks later and then another bombshell or more like a volcano eruption came out of the blue.

"Mr. Jones would like you to come in for an appointment" said the smooth calm voice of the solicitors secretary, "He wants you to understand that there is some urgency to the matter and would tomorrow suit?"

Susan agreed to a 9.30 a.m. appointment wondering what could be the urgency? Surely Mr. Jones could administer her father's simple will in his sleep? After tomorrow plans would go ahead to modernise the pub and think about renting the farm. The rent would bring in a steady income and help to fund the building plans.

"Could I have a glass of water please?"

Susan felt faint and her legs felt like jelly, "Things are not that simple" he said and indeed things couldn't be worse she thought, "the fact of the matter is" droned Mr. Jones, "the debts incurred against your father's estate over the past decade are greater than the value of all the property and assets. The Revenue, the undertaker, the brewery, they all want payment immediately so our advice is to sell the entire assets without delay."

How I would love to slap that self-satisfied expression off his ugly face, she thought when he delivered the final blow, "If you stay on in the house you will be obliged to pay rent."

She had one calendar month to vacate the only home she had ever known.

"What doesn't kill you makes you stronger," her friend Jenny said over and over during the following weeks, "we'll keep a step ahead of them and do what we have to do as quickly as possible."

Jenny's dad was into antiques and had discreetly disposed of her few precious pieces of furniture, two clocks and some antique jewellery before old Jones got there.

They made a pretty sum, Mam had trained her well in survival skills where money was concerned.

Time to go: - finally Susan reached for the old family photo album. She had taken little pleasure in the sorting and putting together of the album but it pleased her mother, and at the time it had relieved the empty drudgery that went on regardless. Carefully she tucked it in alongside the diaries. There was a satisfying dull clunk when she clipped the clasps shut.

The taxi driver juggled the luggage this way and that to fit in the old case alongside the two shiny new Samsonite bags. Susan relaxed half listening to his chatter about the weather and the AA Traffic Watch report. "Will you stop at the post box please Tom?" Susan asked.

The Blue Basildon Bond envelope dropped with a soft thud, inside was a letter accepting a place on a mature student degree course to begin in six weeks' time.

Susan sat back into the car, patted her travel bag and settled herself comfortably for the journey to the airport.

New plans, new beginnings, but before that, Mediterranean cruise here I come.

VERITAS?

Kevin Patrick

"Truth? What is Truth?"

An able administrator queried once. Receiving no right response, he did what was popular and politic in those Bread and Circus days. Ourselves not needing votes, yet requiring the support of the House, are wont to do the same. That's a kind of Truth. Terrorist or Freedom Fighter? Martyr or Heretic? All are true enough for each other.

"What I have written, I have written."

No eyes but mine will ever see these words as I see them now. What is true for me now may not be, a decade hence or a decade since. Truth is a fleeting, passing, changeling thing. So who or what Truth can any trust? No thing and no-one. As Truth lies everywhere. Maybe Truth is really in a shared smile or a grief embraced. In the dawn of a day, without suffering or pain. At the final release. Now there lies a Truth. Quick cover it up! With heavy stone, entombed and silent, or in compact clay with no marker or sign. Yes. Truth Lies.

"You say that I am a King. Yes, but not of this world..."

THE HELLFIRE CLUB

Aisling Doonan

"Is it much further?" Helen huffs and puffs under the weight of her backpack, the metal mug clanking against the side zipper. She keeps getting tangled up in the bars of the camping stool she has strapped to the bottom of the nylon bag. I readjust my own light pack, essentials only, and quickly take a photo of her for posterity.

"No, we're almost there; it's just over the brow of this hill" John replies, turning to give her a cheeky grin "not having second thoughts are we?"

Ben chuckles, his dimples are the deep, speared by a pencil kind, and he knows how to use them to charm. I recognize a charmer when I see one, all warm and seductive on the outside, cold as a digital clock on the inside.

"Not afraid of a few demons and wild cats are you Helen? You can trust us to keep you safe."

"Oh Ben" Amy gave him a playful dig in the arm "Don't tease; you still cry at Disney films, Helen, you're better off sticking with me! I won't let the ghosties get you." Amy giggles and Ben fumes, but they still stay close together as they pick their steps carefully through the loose stones. Helen and John are walking further up the steep muck track side by side; I stay to the rear of the group. Always watchful.

"We used to come up here a lot as kids, we used to play hide and seek in the woods there." John stops for a breather and nods his head towards the spruce, larch and beech.

We all stand and listen for a few moments to their leaves flutter and wave as the breeze wafts through their boughs and mossy trunks. Smaller branches sway, gently slow dancing with an invisible partner. I can see rays of light filled with midges and minute debris hit the forest floor. I can hear nothing now, not even our breathing, except the birdsong, an orchestra of many, all independently chanting. I try to unravel the individual tunes, the robin, the finch, starling and thrush. I lean back against the large rock that is abandoned in the centre of the track. It is the height of a fully grown man and the width of two. I feel the roughness of the granite under my hands as I sink back against the mass. The sunrays hit the ground sharply before a passing cloud brings a chill and the hairs stand up on the back of my neck, a bead of sweat rolls down my temple.

The others are simply staring into the forest. They seem mesmerized by the dappling light flitting from tree to tree. The breeze picks up; its icy fingers caressing our exposed skin, the girls huddle together.

"I think we should go now" Helen is frowning. John picks up on her confusion.

"What's wrong?"

"The birds have stopped singing."

They all raise their ears to the sky, it's amusing to watch, they don't understand.

"Hey Lucy, can you hear anything?" They need some sort of confirmation.

As I open my mouth to reply, the dark cloud obscures the late evening sun and there is a loud sudden crack from behind us. All eyes swivel immediately to where I'm standing and Amy screams. A piercing, tone perfect, *I wish I was an opera singer scream* that leaves my ears stinging.

"Amy, what's wrong?" She's still standing, her mouth gaping, pointing in my general direction. Ben is fussing around her, any excuse to put an arm around her shoulder.

"What is it, did you see something? Please say something Amy, was it the noise you heard?" Ben sounds concerned.

"The, the, the, face, the thing, I saw…" Amy is pointing and her shoulders are vibrating uncontrollably.

"It was a cat, no a thing, no a cat, person, a cat. I saw it, behind the rock." She's still pointing and I'm beginning to feel a little exposed. I walk around the rock.

"There's nothing there Amy, honest, nothing at all, see?" I hold out my arms and smile, "nothing to see at all."

Ben jogs over to the rock and begins to circle it, grinning.

"Legend has it, that if you run around this rock three times backwards, the devil will appear to you" he grins and begins a slow motion backward run. "Will I do it?" Helen squeals, the moment of fear broken and begs him to stop.

"Quit that! We have enough to deal with in the dark tonight without summoning scary stuff to come and get us. Come on, let's get to the summit before the sun sets, I don't want to be setting up camp in the dark."

We begin to move forwards again, keeping tight together, Amy still looking anxiously behind her. Ben keeps a protective hand on her shoulder, guiding her forward. The layers of trees have ended now and we hit the summit of Montpelier Hill, our steps slowing as we take in the great green space in front of us that makes way to the most spectacular view of Dublin below. And there in the centre of the green is the lodge. The Hellfire Club. Its stone walls covered in graffiti, but still an imposing sight standing defiantly against the elements. It was not a welcoming sight, it sits squat and sullen at the very apex of the hill, its side walls extending forward from the stables to enclose the front and enshroud you.

"Well it looks spooky and forbidding enough" Ben surveys the outside of the ruin with John. "Do you think there will be any paranormal activity tonight?"

"I don't know, don't talk it up too much, Amy is nervous enough as it is, this is meant to be a fun camping trip. We don't want to be stuck up here with three hysterical females, we won't get any decent footage then" John looks back to where Helen and Amy are taking photos of the glorious view and then to me, who's standing between the two groups. I smile at him, making myself amenable.

Let's get set up with a fire and something to eat before it gets dark. John takes off his rucksack

"Who's coming in to check out our rooms?"

"I bagsies the en suite" Ben takes a run at the door beating John to it; they disappear inside yahooing and laughing.

"Come on Amy, let's go in and take the tour" Helen gestures and smiles at Amy in encouragement. "You too Lucy, lets stick together, I have a feeling that tonight will be full of adventure."

We stepped over the nettles and overgrown weeds at the door, filing in, Helen first, me watching from the back.

"Do you have your torch? It's kind of darker than I expected." Helen peers into the hallway where the stairs have taken the boys upstairs, the iron banisters smooth from years of traffic. Amy was using her phone as a torch. "Hey look, this must have been the kitchen" she was peering up the large fireplace, twisting to see if she could see daylight "must be blocked," she shrugged.

"Hey ladies" there was a yell from above "You have got to see this" Helen made her way quickly to the stairs, she had turned at the first half landing when Amy noticed the dark room to the back and went to enter it, Helen looking behind her seemed to miss a step and came down heavily on her ankle.

"Ow, ow, ow" she grimaced and sat, not caring about the dirty step, to rub her foot. "I think I've twisted it."

Amy appeared out from the back room, puzzled. "That room is so dark, it's really weird, there's a window, but hardly any light gets through."

Ben appeared over the bannisters "what is taking you lot so long, come on, there's a great view up here and we can set up our sleeping bags in the big room here, lots of space, we could even light a fire in the fireplace. Oh, Helen, what's wrong with your foot?"

"She's twisted it" Amy said as she helped Helen back to her feet and up to the main floor. The view was amazing; Helen even forgot her ankle, as they gazed out over the plains of Dublin, Meath and Kildare. The sun was casting a red and purple glow over the heavy clouds as it set to one side behind us; a fine mist was beginning to creep in over the grass. There was very little noise at this height, there was no birdsong, just the gentle rustle and sway of the trees. The breeze whipped around in circles and then stopped altogether. Swollen clouds came to a stubborn halt over the summit and a chill descended, leaching the day's heat in the shadows.

"Who has the matches?" Ben was busy with the firelighters and had already gathered some sticks to burn. John set up the little primus stove in the corner and soon the delicious aroma of sausages frying made the girls relax a little.

"Look what I found" John was delighted as he came back from foraging with a flat wooden board "Now we have a table, if we rest this on a camping stool; we can use the window ledges to sit on. I brought a pack of cards if anyone is interested?"

"As long as we don't play Poker" Ben sniggered "you know the history of this place". He gave a quick sideways glance at the girls who were busy buttering sandwiches for the sausages.

"I have a feeling that you are going to delight in telling us the gory details" Amy said as she settled herself and her food on the little camping stool in front of the makeshift dining table. She took some cans of beer from her backpack and looked back at Ben defiantly.

"You can't scare me now, even if we are in a haunted house at night and its pitch black outside."

There was a high pitched shrill scream from somewhere close by, its timing was impeccable; Amy dropped her beer, its contents foamed and sudsed sadly across the floor.

"It's just a fox" Helen said.

"Or the ghost of the woman who was rolled down the hill to her death in a burning barrel. Can you smell the smoke?" Ben joked.

"No, that's just the sausages burning, quick save them" Helen playfully jabbed John in the ribs.

Tendrils of mist curled around the window openings, leaving everyone feeling damp as they huddled closer to the fire. I was the only one left to sit in the windowsill but I was content.

"Is it wise to stay here? We will perish with the cold" Helen's teeth were chattering. John stood to look out the window.

"It's too misty now, we'd never make it back to Tallaght in that, and we'd lose our way or get knocked down on the road. Better if we wait until it lifts. Maybe dawn."

"I doubt we'll sleep now, how about a game of cards, keep us occupied for a few hours" Ben was already shuffling the deck in his hands eagerly.

Everyone drifted back to their places at the table, bats swooped outside with inaudible squeaks, the cards were dealt and I sat up straight, focused on the table.

"But we have no money to bet with" Amy looks puzzled.

"How about, the loser has to sleep alone, in the other room" Ben chuckles.

The cards are dealt and the fire burns low. Within ten minutes Helen unhappily folds. She goes to lay her hand on the table when she yelps and her hands fly to her throat.

"My necklace, something yanked it off, I think it's on the floor" rubbing her neck she peeps under the board and drops to her knees to use her hands to feel for it.

I watch with glorious anticipation, my time has come. All Hell is about to break loose. Helen's hands pat the ground, her head low, visibility is nonexistent. The embers are dying in the corner as Helen finally reaches my feet. Or should I say cloven hooves.

THE LOST NIGHT

Margaret Maguire

"Hello!" she shouted. As she waved her two hands in his direction.

He looked across the street. And his gaze met a stranger. 'Who is that woman?' he thought. He stared after her back. Tall, blonde, long legs, high heels. Wearing a short summer dress. 'Not bad' he thought. But where had he seen her before? Or more importantly where had she seen him?

He went through all the haunts of the last month, ending with the night before. Oh God no. Don't let it be the night before.

He had gone to the pub early to meet the lads. A few pints were had. Then they decided to go in to the night-club, well decided was the wrong word. They had staggered in and crawled out. As his friend Colin would say. He couldn't remember a thing today. He had woken up at noon. Thank God it was Sunday. His father gave him a look, from behind the newspaper. His mother came right out with it. "What time did you get in last night?" "Ah it wasn't too late," he said sheepishly.

But he still couldn't remember. Now strange women were greeting him in the street. 'Why?' kept echoing through his mind.

He turned the corner and went into Reilly's shop for the paper. In the doorway he bumped into Nell Kelly.

"Ah the hard man" she said as she slapped him on the shoulder and gave him a broad wink as she rushed off down the street. 'Ah please, no' he thought. Now the old ones were pleased to see him. Nell must be at least forty, and worse still she frequented Murphy's pub. He bought his paper, and sat on the seat outside the shop, keeping his head down pretending to read. His thoughts were hurting his head now.

So he decided to call Colin. He rang the house, his mother answered. Her quick, sharp, "Yes" sent alarm bells through his muddled brain. In a soft low voice he asked "Is Colin there?"

The loud "No" and the slamming down of the phone, was a further indication that Colin was in trouble. Whatever happened last night it must have been serious.

As he raised his head, he spotted Amy walking towards him.

He didn't know her second name. She was known to the male population as Amy. She came bouncing down the footpath. The belt that she wore as a skirt was putting a strain on her hips. Her knee length boots were beating a rhythm on the concrete, the three colours of her hair fighting for dominance in the sun. He could see her mouth work the chewing gum, even from a distance.

"Hi" she called as she slowed her step.

"Oh Hi" he said in as low a tone as he could manage.

She slowed down, as she approached. "Well?" she asked, as she peered at him, through several layers of mascara, as she chewed her gum, and smiled a half smile. She didn't wait for an answer, just swaggered off, down the street. It was a knowing swagger. She knew something, it was written all over her. He walked home as fast as he could.

As he walked past the open kitchen door his mother came out. "What's the matter with you?" she asked "You look terrible. Where were you last night?"

"Oh just went to Murphy's for a while" he said as he climbed the stairs.

He went into his room and sat on the bed. If only he could remember. Something must have happened last night, because there was young ones waving at him, old ones winking at him, and Amy peering at him suggestively.

The one thing he was sure of was 'never again'. He was finished with drink.

He could never have a day like this again.

THE TROLL'S TOOTH

Kevin Patrick

When the Troll was small, well small for a young Troll anyway, being about a fathom tall, his first tiny Troll tooth began to come loose. This is no surprise really, as Trolls mostly munch on the bones of the dead, so all that cracking and crunching and scrunching and munching is bound to have an effect. Even on the teeth of a Troll.

Well, one night, young Troll was munching away when his front left incisor first wobbled, then wibbled, then fell out. How young Troll howled and jumped up in surprise, as this was the first time it had ever happened to him. He ran to Mommy Troll all silky tears and green blood.

Now Troll tears are made of sulphuric acid which would scar the skin of you and me, but Trolls have very thick skin, thicker than old leather bound books or the bark of knarled ancient trees, so he didn't feel it. But he felt something worse, the fear of something new.

"Oh Mommy, Oh Mommy Me!" howled young Troll as he could not understand what had taken place and he was ever-frightened of all things new or unexpected.

Now some say that Trolls have hearts of stone and no feelings at all for anyone but themselves, along with their thick skins. This is not true at all.

Yes, they have thick skins, but do you know they need them, as they are jeered at and avoided by most, on account of their grotesque and hideous appearance.

However, they do possess hearts of blood and shed true tears with honest feelings, just like you and me. So Mommy Troll explained to young Troll that Baby Troll teeth must fall out, so that bigger, stronger teeth can come through, so there is really nothing to be frightened of.

"But what about dis tiddler?" lisped young Troll holding his bloody loose tooth aloft. "Waddle I do widdit?"

Now as you can imagine, there is no Tooth Fairy collecting service for Trolls, as not even the Fairy Folk will come near them on account of their appearance.

So Mommy Troll said, "Here my boy, take this tinder box I just found and put your tiddler tooth in it. Now at midnight on the next full moon, bury this at the clearing in the Wylde Wood of Woe, on top of Drumlin Hill."

"I will" said young Troll "but wot'll happen to it?"

"Well" said his kindly mother, as she looked into his trusting eyes through her own ancient watery beautiful eyes, thinking for a minute.

"Well, Old Radharc the Badger of the Sett will collect the tooth just after the full moon, as he visits there once a Moon-Month to collect any Troll Teeth left there, to put towards a necklace he is making for his wife Brocaí. In return," Mommy paused, "he will leave three fresh hares for you, for eating and wearing, one Moon-Month later."

"Oh!" young Trolls eyes glazed over with happiness, the true happiness of the young. He loved hare skin. So soft, against the roughness of his own.

Well, at the next full moon, just two nights after at the Wylde Wood of Woe, young Troll lolloped up Drumlin Hill. His heart singing with his long arms swinging, the tinder box in his rough hands. He was lolloping along so gaily that the tooth worked loose from the box and fell unheard and unseen by young Troll before he reached the burying spot.

Young Troll dug quick and true as all Trolls can, *(on account of their diet)* and he held the tinder box in his leathery hands lovingly over the freshly dug earth for a moment.

"Shall I just have a peep?" he said to himself "of my ickle tooth, soon to be made towards a necklace for Brocaí?"

He looked around him as if for an answer. Then he thought 'No, might be bad luck n'all.' So into the ground went the tinder box and was covered in the moment it takes for a cloud to whistle past the moon.

Which is just what young Troll did, as he lollagalloped back down the Hill through the woods, returning home to dream of the softness of hare skin.

From nearby, stood stone still, like a statue, a pair of ancient watery eyes watched him silently, with that self-same tooth, softly held in a pair of skin-cracked hands.

One Moon-Month later at the next full moon and well, what do you know?

Ah! Yes. Three beautiful brown hares freshly laid out, right at the spot where the tinder box was buried by young Troll only the Moon-Month before, were found now, by himself.

And Look! A little sapling has sprung up at that very spot too.

Young Troll took his three soft hares away to feast on and to wear, but in all his joy and jollity he stopped for a moment, as if he had just thought of something or someone. He ran straight to his mother.

"Oh Mommy, Mommy look, look!" he held up his booty "I'm not scared no more Mommy, of falling teeth. Look what Old Radharc left me just like you said, come on Mommy, I will share them with you."

Mommy Troll smiled through her watery eyes, and said she would fashion him a lovely hare skin sling.

"Oh Mommy" beamed young Troll "just the thing!"

HIS WORLD

Lionel Mullally

At fifty-two years of age, Peter Daly was often described as a career civil servant. He wasn't.

He was a civil servant but was not career orientated and had been in his Executive Officer role for twenty four years. Several younger members that he had trained in, supervised and mentored had progressed along the ranks and moved to other sections or departments. Peter hadn't.

He'd smile and say "I'm happy as I am!"

Some of the younger ladies in the office thought him older than his years.

"He dresses old," said one, "who wears Farah slacks these days?"

Peter always dressed for his office role in standard shirt, tie and trousers. He was never flamboyant. Perhaps, a Santa tie at Christmas.

He was polite, friendly, yet private, smiling and always helpful. He was, in a word, nice. And so, therefore, was often the subject of casual humour at his expense.

"Coming on the beer tonight with us Peter?" they'd

ask, smiling, knowing the standard answer, and miming the words behind him.

"No thanks. A night in with the missus and the soaps and some reading beckons. Another time perhaps."

"That wife of his has a tight rein on him" they'd whisper. "God love him, he's got no life at all with her."

At five thirty Peter would tidy his desk and bid the others goodnight. He'd gather his coat around him, place his newspaper and lunchbox in his ecofriendly carrier bag and depart for home.

"He'd be great in a quiz, wouldn't he?" suggested a colleague, "he must be an expert on the soaps, books and TV!"

"He wouldn't go to one in the first place" was the answer, "Probably wouldn't be allowed! A few hours at the Christmas do and the same at a retirement function is all he's permitted! And you never see his missus with him."

They chuckled and readied for home.

Peter walked the half mile to the bus stop, waited and boarded his bus. He sat on the left near the back, among some familiar faces, nodding and smiling as he did. After thirty minutes he alighted at his stop, turned left and walked through a narrow lane, emerging onto a quiet cul-de-sac. At the fourth house he opened the gate, promising himself to oil the hinge that addressed him, and walked in the twelve steps. Sliding open the porch door, he removed the key from his pocket and, opening the front door with it, entered home. He placed his bag at the foot of the stairs on his left and walked further in to disarm the alarm. He returned to close the door and pick up the post from the floor. He looked through the envelopes as he walked into the kitchen and, in a practiced move, filled the kettle, turned it on to boil and turned on the TV in the sitting room.

For the next hour he prepared and ate his dinner, drank two mugs of tea, scanned the news on Teletext and laughed quietly to a comedy programme on the screen. At ten minutes to the hour he washed all and put away his mug and plate to their spaces. He put on his coat and placed the book, 'Jo Nesbo's The Snowman,' in his bag, set the alarm and left.

The walk took just over half an hour. As he entered through the automatic doors of the building he opened his coat zip and felt the heat greet him.

"Good evening ladies" he said, "how are you today?"

Smiling back, they'd answer and he would enquire after a named son or daughter or husband.

"I'll talk to you later," and he'd finish with, "best not be late for Coronation Street."

He'd take his leave of them and walk the hall, his steps echoing slightly in the emptiness. He'd pause, knock gently and open the door, entering the room.

"It's only me."

He walks to the side of the bed and reaching over, gently kisses his wife's brow. He moves a stray hair, looks again and smiles.

"Hello love," he whispers.

Turning, he removes his coat and hangs it by the door and takes his seat beside her.

"I haven't missed anything I hope" he continues, and reaches to collect the remote and turn the volume up on the TV. He reaches over to hold her hand. They watch in silence. Peter would exclaim or show surprise at a turn in the show, point out an interesting moment or laugh at the latest witty remarks from one of the characters. Peter tells her of the day's events at work; of Paul and Claire in the office and a deadline missed; of the news from his mother in Dublin; of the latest in the news on the papers. The steady breathing from his wife and muted beeping are the only response.

At 9pm, Nurse Elaine calls in with a student and greets Peter. They know each other well and are relaxed and comfortable companions. Reading the monitors and taking notes she talks, asks after his work, tells of the first steps her grandchild has taken, and the first bruises from the first fall. They share a few more stories, comment on the weather and the hopes for the county team.

Peter had read of the last match and Elaine mentioned watching it in the freezing cold from the stands as her nephew had made the county panel.

Elaine helps Peter to freshen the pillows and settle his wife. As she leaves Peter removes the book from his bag.

She pauses and watches as he takes the marker from its page and settles again asking,

"Now, where were we? Ah yes, the scary bit!"

He thumbs a page and continues to read to his wife from where he had left off.

"Who's that man?" asked the student nurse to Elaine as they continued their rounds.

"Peter Daly," she replies, "a lovely man. He was a great comfort to me two years ago when my husband Dan passed away. He has been coming here for years. He's here every night at the same time to watch the TV with his wife and read her a book. He stays with her till almost eleven o clock most nights"

"Is she getting better?"

"No, unfortunately not and she never will. She's been like that for twenty one years now. A road collision. Her brain stem is severed from the spinal cord. It can never repair. Her body continues to breathe and the cardiac and respiratory systems are fine, but she is not conscious and never will be, conscious again."

"Oh that's terrible. But why does he come every night? I don't mean to sound cruel, but she wouldn't know. She doesn't know him anymore."

Elaine smiled.

He was asked that once and he replied, "But I know who she is."

"He never misses a night with her. I heard too from his sister, that, just before the accident, his wife had joked that if he really loved her he'd shout it out to the world. He reached over and whispered in her ear 'I love you'. When she asked why he didn't shout it out for the world to hear, he replied that she was his world."

They continued their round. Later, Peter marked the page of the book and placed it in his bag.

As he freshened the pillows once more and straightened the sheets he spoke of the new person in the office, that they were related to an old neighbour of theirs, of the talk of the changes that the new Minister would make in the department.

"But, haven't we heard all that before! Now, I best let you get some rest."

Reaching in till their foreheads touched for several seconds, his eyes remained closed as he whispered "I love you." He remained close and still for a few seconds more.

"I'll see you tomorrow."

He left the room and quietly closed the door. On the way out he said goodnight to Elaine and the other nurses. He walked home and entered the house again as earlier. He turned the TV on and caught the last of a film that he silently promised to get on DVD sometime. He prepared for and settled into bed.

He awoke at his usual time of six thirty the following morning. He rose and dressed to walk for almost an hour, exchanging waves and salutes with the familiar likeminded others before returning to breakfast, shower and dress for work. As he entered the office he smiled a morning greeting to Paul who commented on the nights events in the pub.

"Did you go out yourself Peter?"

"Ah no. Watched TV and chatted with herself mostly. Some funny bits on the TV and told her all about yourself and Claire's mishap on the project. Quiet enough otherwise."

Paul nodded. He turned and asked Peter if he would help him with his application form for the promotion role that had been advertised.

"I'll go for it" said Paul; "I think I'd like the role, and the move. Six years here is long enough for me."

"No problem" answered Peter, "bring the form in later and I'll go through it with you."

The day, like other days, continued its familiar rhythm.

THE PHONE CALL

Helen Corcoran

"Here we are!" Dan said, unnecessarily, as they reached the last flight of stairs. He was out of breath, a trickle of sweat made its way down between his shoulder blades and his limbs were aching. He slowly stood with his back to the cold cement wall until his breathing became steady again. Liz, his wife of forty-three years, walked ahead to their apartment door, calling back to him to hurry up and that she was putting the kettle on.

Realizing that he was still holding the two overflowing shopping bags he dropped them with a thud onto the cement floor. Their contents crashed out, cans rolling, milk spilling and mixing in with the spilt flour as it slowly flowed towards the top step. Dan just stood starring at the mess. Liz in the distance was calling him that the kettle had boiled and that she needed the groceries so that they could have the chocolate biscuits with their tea.

Dan turned around, putting his right hand in his pocket and enclosed his fingers around its contents. Feeling its smoothness it gave him the courage he craved. He headed down the stairs.

"For the last time," he thought.

He ran, taking two steps at a time, nearly colliding with an elderly lady, but side stepped just in time.

As he pushed open the exit door, the bright sunshine caused him to blink. Standing for a moment he looked around at the familiar grey apartment blocks, the small garden surrounded by concrete, the clothes hanging on small clothes lines on small landings and the small corner shop.

'No more' he thought.

He focused on the task ahead as he walked on without looking back. As he passed the corner shop, he could hear Liz calling his name, but he didn't turn back. His step quickened.

Liz frantically opened the window calling out Dan's name. She looked down to the ground level but he wasn't there. She ran back to the stairs and gazed at the mess on the floor. Two distinctive footprints covered in flour heading down the stairs. She followed them down and out into the open. But there was no sign of him. She knocked on the door of the ground floor apartment but there was no answer.

"Where is he?"

"Dan," she shouted again, much louder this time.

Still there was no sign of him.

"What will I do?"

Liz went back upstairs, the twelve flights, no wonder Dan kept complaining about that. As she was nearing their apartment the phone was ringing. She dashed in and picked up the receiver.

"Hello"

"Liz, it's me," Dan said.

"Where are you?"

"Just listen" he paused a moment, "I've had enough, those bloody stairs, no more and and...Never mind..." Silence.

The silence was broken by Dan saying, "Goodbye Liz."

The phone went dead in her ear.

MERGING TRAFFIC

Aisling Doonan

"Tonight's the night" Sinead squeals with ill-concealed excitement. She is five foot nothing, perfectly petite in her yoga gear and wearing a hanger around her neck to demonstrate how wonderful the little black dress, that she has brought for Emma, is. She pulls at the jersey fabric and bats her eyelids coquettishly a few times.

"Sure, how could he not ask, when you look like this?"

"But I won't look like you" Emma says "I'll be the slightly taller, more rotund version, that dress scares me, it wants to throw me out on stage and whistle at me. Why can't I go in my jeans and blazer?"

"Absolutely not! Anyway, aren't you wearing that corset pull me in, pop me out thing?" Jennifer thrust a pair of five inch killer heels with a tiny insignificant strap into Emma's hands." Try these on," she stood back to survey with a critical eye.

"Yes, but I'm not sure it will work. It looks dangerous, like being wrapped up by a boa constrictor. I'll never be able to eat my dinner; the posh restaurant will be wasted on me."

Jennifer ignored her, her eyes busily calculating the parts of Emma's person that needed the most work.

"Hmmm, you'll need eyelashes."

Emma was aghast, "I have eyelashes" she whimpered.

"Yes, but they don't have enough 'oomph,' you need total impact tonight, these photos will be on your mantelpiece…for life."

The way she said it, made Emma wonder if that was a good thing. She bit back a retort as to why she would want a photo of a stranger on her mantelpiece gathering dust unto eternity.

"Now, I have some goodies for you, you can thank me later" Sinead untangled herself smoothly from the hanger and dress, to pull several little boxes and packages from her 'Mary Poppins' bag.

"There are relaxing bath salts, a brightening face masque and super hydrating hair conditioner. So you can have a long luxurious bath and prep and be nice and relaxed for dinner with Rob this evening." She lined up the products on the dressing table and pointed to each one in turn with an eyeliner pencil.

"Oh, and you'll need these too," popping the box of black spidery curls at the end. Sinead must have caught Emma frowning at them "They're false eyelashes Em!" She scowled. "How did you get to be so clueless?"

Jennifer stood, and gathered her coat while Sinead, shook her perfectly coiffed head in disbelief, before Emma could reply.

"Now remember, pamper then prep and good luck, we'll be waiting for your happy text."

They both disappeared into a cloud of translucent powder and Chanel No 5.

Emma sighed, it was 4.00 p.m. and Rob was calling to collect her at 8.00 p.m. sharp to bring her to one of the most expensive restaurants in town. It had a twelve month waiting list and a name that could not be pronounced. She was sure she wouldn't even be able to read the menu, let alone appreciate the rich food and the thoughts of Rob asking her an important question left her stomach on spin cycle. She looked at the long line of unfamiliar products on her dressing table and picked a random bottle to begin her ablutions.

As she washed her hair with Jennifer's Mane and Tail shampoo, she remembered the look of horror on Jennifer's face when she asked her if she had picked it up at the vets. Grinning, she added the hydrating hair mask that promised locks that Kate Middleton would envy. As she massaged the bubblegum scented lotion into her hair, she imagined Kate ransacking the shelves in the Queen's stables for her secret hair products stash. She wrapped it all up into a warm fluffy towel and moved onto applying the face mask. The clay was cold and smelled of damp earth. She smoothed it on as best she could, idly wondering if she would be able to plaster the cracks in the ceiling with it too. Finally, she had smoothed a layer over her chin, cheeks, forehead and nose in a perfect oval. Already it was beginning to harden and she couldn't smile or wiggle her nose.

Emma read the box of bath salts, as she ran the steaming water into the tub. It promised to leave her glowing with youth and vitality, detoxed, hydrated and de-stressed. It sounded like the perfect balm to her anxiousness. She sprinkled a generous grey heap into the bath and watched it clump and sink unhelpfully. Maybe all this preparation was adding a layer of stress rather than joy. Referring back to the instructions Emma realized that she was supposed to steam open her pores to gain the most from the seaweed extract. She carefully added a kettleful of boiling water to the sink. Steam rose and mingled with the salty fishy smell from the bath. She was suddenly ravenous for a battered cod and chips doused in vinegar and hoped the scent of Bundoran would have dissipated before this evening. Her hand squeaked against the mirror as she cleaned a spot to see her face. A ghostly clay effigy stared back at her, cracking and powdery at the edges.

"Oh no, I didn't leave it on too long, did I?" Emma blanched as she scrunched her face and felt the hardened clay pinch and crinkle. Absent mindedly she cupped her hands in the sinkful of water to swish it over her face.

"Owwwwww" Emma's hands roared in protest and sprang back, the heat of the water magically turning them into garnet throbbing flesh sticks. They pulsed and in her shock she stared at them for a moment or two before attempting to empty the sink and run the cold tap to soothe her bitten fingers. Not the easiest thing to do when they are swollen and your expensive French manicure has been laid to waste.

Bath next; she gingerly dipped a toe in before dropping down into the grey oily water. The powdered seaweed extract stuck to her skin and she hoped this meant she would absorb all of its organic goodness. Emma settled herself, neck resting on the edge of a rolled up facecloth, and closed her eyes. Her hands were weightless and tingled dully when she moved them. The briny scent soon had her floating and bobbing off in a little sleepy raft. Outside the torrential rain showed no sign of stopping. The sky was uniform grey and the steady tip tap of drops against the window was soothing. She dreamt of being buried alive in a sandpit and awoke with a gasp, cold and shriveled with a hardened mask of concrete. She tried to pick it off and winced as each tiny slab she tried to remove obstinately refused to budge.

"Don't panic" Emma told herself as she wrapped a warmed towel around herself. The mirror showed a patchy red and white chalky clown face.

"What have I done?" Emma's throat began to sting and her eyes reddened further with hot tears. She turned on the light to inspect the damage and discovered a grey tinge ending at the high water mark at her neck.

"I look like a Gremlin! Oh Jennifer, you need to get over here now" Emma wailed into the phone "please, and bring…products."

Ten minutes later Emma was being soothed by warm hands and a comforting monologue of nice things.

"Think fluffy white kittens, no calorie chocolate, five day weekends, free bar at a wedding, no hangover wine, 99% sale in Brown Thomas, Tom Hiddleston as James Bond."

She patted her down, scrubbed her with olive oil and sugar to try and get rid of her gremlin skin and picked the last few clay scabs off Emma's face. Jennifer dried her wrinkled hair and brushed it until it gleamed smoothly under the lights.

"You almost look presentable now" she smiled, "still a little grey but you can barely tell, especially under mood lighting."

Emma quickly got dressed and finished her make-up with only seconds to spare before the doorbell rang. Rushing down the hall finally smiling to open the door, she barely registered the snapping noise before the high heel strap broke and the side of her foot made painful contact with the wooden floor.

The front door was opened with little grace and all Rob could see was a woman whose face looked like she had given a winning lottery ticket to her ex-best friend. She was standing on one leg and holding a shoe.

"Cinderella?" He smiled weakly, the collar of his shirt suddenly tight.

"Your carriage awaits, my lady" he crooked his elbow towards her hopefully and gestured towards the waiting taxi.

"I need to change my shoes"

Rob watched as she limped down the hall. "Are you ok Emma? You look a little green; did you hurt your foot?" Emma returned several inches shorter and happier looking.

"Yes, I'm fine now, twisted my ankle, that's all. Let's go."

Emma was fizzing with happy anticipation. She took a deep breath and gathered her wrap and bag. Her perfect gentleman opened the door and ushered her into the taxi. Finally sitting down, the corset that promised to keep her all in, threatened to throw the contents of her stomach out. It bit into her sides and she was afraid if she tipped over she might fall out. Her ankle throbbed and her boiled fingers were still a bit tender.

"You look beautiful"

Rob turned to her as the taxi driver took off, squeezing her hand before snatching it away and rubbing it frantically on the back seat upholstery. He was fidgety and uncharacteristically quiet. Usually he would be telling her a funny story from work or news from his large family. She watched him from under her ridiculous new lashes; his hand flew up to his collar to unbutton it. Emma noticed the arms on his suit were too long. Smiling to herself she wondered if he had also put in an afternoon of friendly advice and borrowed clothes.

Rob tried hard to sit still, his top lip was threatening to turn into a waterfall and he was sure his collar was trying to choke him. He fiddled with his button and then realized that his hand was also beginning to sweat. He was afraid to rub them on his borrowed trousers in case he left streaks. He thought he saw Emma wince when he had taken her hand, she didn't look well, and she was a funny colour. He was also suddenly ravenous, fish and chips sounded like a better idea than snails in garlic or whatever the new restaurant was going to offer. He had such a longing he could almost smell the sea.

Five minutes later as they hit the dual carriageway, there was a gravelly pop and the taxi wobbled slightly before pulling over into the hard shoulder.

"Can I ask you to step out of the vehicle please, so that I can change the tyre? I'm very sorry, it won't take long. Can you wear these?" He offered them two enormous Hi-Vis yellow vests.

They stood huddled together, at the side of the road, under acres of luminous yellow polyester and surrounded by glowing triangles. Rob held Emma close to keep her warm. Traffic whizzed by as the taxi man worked, deftly removing wheel nuts and removing the damaged wheel. Emma felt a cold sting on her forehead as the first hail stone fell and bounced down the front of her dress, she squealed as the ice melted against her skin. Within seconds they were being pelted with military precision, making them dance and screech like children on a sugar high. Laughing at the side of the road, plucked, polished, pummeled, manicured and buffed till every inch looked like it belonged to someone else, wearing other people's clothes, Emma and Rob finally began to feel like themselves. Bedraggled, glowing in the dark, with the taxi man as a witness, Rob bent at the knee and produced a little wooden box from his pocket just as the rain began.

"Emma would you do me the honour..."

Diesel fumes caught in the back of Emma's throat and her eyes began to water, she managed to cough an encouragement for Rob to continue.

"...of cancelling our dinner reservation and..."

Tears were spilling out of Emma's eyes, her throat was on fire, and one of her false lashes was hanging on by a single spider leg and obscuring her vision. She closed her mouth tight, hoping that the cough would be contained and simply go away but instead it exploded out her nose instead as Rob took a large breath.

"Emma, will you..."

An articulated lorry roared past, its horn blaring and a tsunami wave of dirty water in its wake drenching the happy couple and the taxi driver who was quietly weeping into a dirty rag.

TRUE EMPATHY

Kevin Patrick

If I were you and you were me
then we'd have true empathy.
If just for one earth's axis spin
we lived inside each other's skin.

We each other, for just one day
random thoughts the things we say.
The secret fears, the spoken voice
the daily choosing thousandth choice.

The ebb and flowing of the day,
bargains won to avoid affray.
To truly see, as I see you
how you see me, the way you do.

To swap man for wife and wife for man
to be part of each other's plan.
To be you, and you be me
feel as you, as each other see.

How similar-different we really are
how strange familiar our thinking's are.
How many things we still don't know
about ourselves we chose to show.

And when the earth its axis spun
to ourselves return with the rising sun.
Like seeping tide on stranded shores
we wouldn't need to speak at all.

As we would now each other know
what we feel and why we show.
Our many faces our varied ways
to each other across the days.

I in you and you in me
then we'd have True Empathy.

THE LATE LAMENTED

Margaret Maguire

The night she left him on the floor had started like most nights. She had come from work, and had her dinner. Liver, she loved liver. She had made some soup the day before, with bones. Yes, she loved bones. There was a lot you could do with bones.

He had come in and she had heated up some Irish Stew for him. She left him in the kitchen enjoying it and went upstairs. When she came back down there he was stretched on the floor. She put on her coat and went down to Mulcaheys.

They were all there, the usual lot. The ones who whispered when she came in, the ones too deep in conversation to notice her, the ones who tried not to look at her. Yes they were all there. Tim, the barman, came over.

"Well, what's it to be tonight Carmel?" he asked.

She had to think for a while "I will have a Bloody Mary" she said. After she drank the Bloody Mary she still didn't feel calm. So she thought she would treat herself again. "Hi Tim" she called "I will have a whiskey, make it a double." She drank the double then headed home, deep in thought.

He would still be on the floor of course. She had made sure of that. But the kitchen floor was no place for him. She would have to move him. She had not thought the situation through. He had to pay, that was all she had thought about. He had got away with things long enough.

It had come to a head a month ago. She had gone in to work and found them in the kitchen.

They were all there. The one who eyed her every time she passed, the one who quickened her step when she entered a room, the one who carefully removed the carving knives from the kitchen drawer every morning, and placed them carefully in a lock press with the office folders. Why you would need carving knives for paperwork she would never know. Not only were they all there, they were all gossiping about her and him.

Kate was saying in her high pitched voice. "I'd kill him if it were me."

And Dot was saying "I'd have nothing to do with him in the first place. You would think that even she could do better."

That was when she decided that things had to change. She went into the canteen and had a bowl of Scotch broth. She liked Scotch broth; you could mix a lot of things in there.

When she went home she made a nice pot of Irish Stew. He liked Irish Stew. She always liked to add a pinch of her own herbs just to make it special. He devoured a large dish full, and asked for more.

Of course, this fellow had lasted longer than the last fellow. That poor man had a serious accident one lively Saturday morning. She had taken away all the sharp knives after that. Just for safety. To guard against enquiring minds. Minds like that can be a dangerous thing.

So this fellow had the freedom of her lovely kitchen, with no sharp instruments to injure himself on. But of course he couldn't behave himself. Didn't appreciate how lucky he was.

She hadn't even asked him to go out to the wood shed, to chop some wood for her. Like the fellow before the last fellow.

That was when he had that accident with the axe. Oh an axe can be a dangerous thing if you hold it in the wrong position.

Now here she was again with this fellow lying on the kitchen floor. Went and dropped dead. Of course he did eat a lot of stew.

But that shouldn't kill anyone. She sat down at the table to consider her next move. Yes, tomorrow she might have Devilled Kidneys for dinner.

A JAR OF PICKLED ONIONS

Kevin Patrick

There's Poetry
in a Jar of Pickled Onions
on my shelf
small and sweet all silverskin
in the cupboard by the delph.

The ingredients are several
printed clearly as they ought to
Onions, Spirit Vinegar,
Malt Barley and some Water,
with Sodium Meta-bi-sulphíte
just in case you're wondering
to preserve those sacred silverskins
to avoid an onion sundering.

On the label are instructions.
How to store this fine munition
a Customer Care Helpline
and some figures on nutrition.

SCRÍOBH SCRIBBLES

They swirl around when picked up
in their happy carefree brine
the tang of tickled onions
and their pickled onion lives
is leaking, from the fastened jar
despite it being tight closed
as surely as the relish
of the spirit hits my nose.

They're peeled and oh so tasty
so sweet and yet so tangy
being totally delicious
buried in a turkey sandwich.

And yet, I'm not just here to praise
their pickled onion flavour.
I'm here to find the Poetry
that just might be my saviour.

For the onions at the top can move
around now, oh so freely
but the onions at the bottom
don't have a life so easy
supporting all the others
so the ones above are free
whilst those below are smothered
by the Top Society.

My God! There goes a Metaphor;
this must be Poetry
despite the rhyme and metre
of this simple grocery.

There's Poetry: almost everywhere,
you simply have to look
away from screens, distractions
and that dusty old Poem Book.

For then you'll find that Poetry
is sitting on the shelf
exuding barley vinegar
in the cupboard by the delph.

ST. JOSEPH'S MAN

Lionel Mullally

Peter Keenan breathed through an open mouth as he walked slowly up the slight incline into his parish church, the Church of the Sacred Heart, situated at the end of the town. It had been his parish church for all of his sixty three years. The large oaken door was open, inviting him in and, pushing the smaller internal door with its frosted glass, he entered. The door swung slowly and silently to a close behind him shutting out the life noises of the small country town.

Removing his cap he walked up the central aisle, turned right at the halfway mark and followed the smaller aisle to the right corner of the church in front of the statue and candle rack. The coins in his hand were slotted in and the votive candle chosen and placed in the middle of the middle row. The empty remains of two other tea-light candles were on opposing ends and rows. Taking the box of matches from the side he scratched one into life, let the first flare ease and held it over his candle until the wick caught and the bright spark and hiss released the wax burning smell bringing his prayer to life. He stepped back and removed the weathered leather pouch from his pocket and spilled the Rosary beads into his right hand. He sat on the seat in the second row, put his cap on the left beside him, allowed his breathing to settle and focused on the candle as it brought light and shadows to the statue of Saint Joseph.

He was alone in the church.

The red glow from the Sanctuary Lamp on the altar told him God was there. He blessed himself with the beads, kissing the cross to finish, and started the Our Father and continued. He looked up to the statue of Saint Joseph as he prayed. Joseph was his favourite. He was the one he went to at times like this. Joseph always helped. Granted, the others were good too and he'd no problem with them, but Joseph was his man. The pleading and bleeding eyes of the Sacred Heart never called to him and the distant eyes to Heaven of the Pietas Madonna never met his. St Anthony always looked a bit watery to him, staring off into space like that, and Holy Nuns were alien to him.

But Joseph he knew and understood; a working man, a husband, a father. He always felt Joseph was taken for granted too and just put in the corner of the church and crib. Saint Joseph understood him and would intercede for him.

"I'm sure he wasn't a Saint till he died," Peter had told his family often enough.

"He didn't go around all pious and blessed and holy looking with work to be done. He'd have lost the rag with the young Jesus the odd time, his mollycoddling mother, the perfect holy in-laws that always thought she could have done better. Not to mention the difficult customers demanding a cheaper price when a promised build or furniture was made."

Joseph understood him. When he asked him for help he was never let down. Yes, sometimes what he had wanted had taken a couple of weeks or months longer than he had hoped or planned for, but wasn't that tradesmen the world over! He continued to thread the beads through his fingers, pausing at the break in the link to finish the decade with the Fatima prayer of;

'O my Jesus, forgive us our sins, save us from the fires of hell, lead all souls to Heaven, especially those who have most need of your mercy.'

He moved to the Third Mystery and remembered his reason for being there, closed his eyes and bowed his head. He opened them as his prayer ended to watch his offerings golden flame flicker and extinguish, the wax pooling in its circle and the grey smoke from his candle curling towards heaven, bringing his cares with it, and the weight and worries of the day.

Joseph knew him. Not the saint, but the man. 'God was love' he'd been told, but Joseph was one of us, a man, just like him. He'll sort it!

He placed his beads in their pouch and returned them to their pocket. He took his cap as he stood. He nodded a thanks and a goodbye to Joseph and edged from the seat. He walked back along the aisle, pausing at the centre to bend the knee slightly to genuflect before the altar.

He had nothing against God, he just didn't know Him.

As he left through the door and emerged into the life of the town, he switched his cap to his left hand and touched the tip of his fingers in the font's water; blessing himself quickly and placing his cap on in the one practiced and fluid motion, and started for home.

He'd leave all to Joseph. He knew he would sort it out for him.

WINDOW

Helen Corcoran

"Will this be the day?" she thought as she pressed her pale face against the dirty window pane. Sara just about reached it by getting up on her tip toes, but she liked the feel of the cold glass against her skin, and it was close to the outside world. Every day she hoped that maybe a passer-by might see her face there or hear her calling out, but they never did.

Sara slowly turned away and slumped to the floor. It was covered in a dark brown, dirty carpet and the walls at one time were covered with wallpaper, which had faded so much, the original colour was unrecognisable. She was cold and hungry and needed to go to the bathroom. In the last couple of days, she had reverted to using the far corner of the room to do so, as the customary bathroom visit had not happened for some days now. It just added to all the other smells. Slowly getting up she moved towards the corner, and as she passed the door, she tried the handle, but it was locked. No toilet paper.

It was one hundred and twenty seven days since she was brought here, by whom? She still did not know, and 'why?' is a bigger mystery to her.

Sara was walking home from work that fateful evening when a black SUV screeched and blocked her way. Shocked into immobility as the door flung open and two big men dressed in black jumped out and grabbed her, covering her head with a bag and roughly bundled her onto the back seat. As the vehicle moved off the men restrained her hands and feet.

Food and water was delivered every day, and Sara was allowed to use the bathroom facilities, but the man always accompanied her, even though her head was covered with the bag. She was so grateful to get to the bathroom, although being humiliated, she put up with him being there. Speaking only to give her orders he never made conversation with her.

Recently his visits became less frequent and Sara was rationing her food and water. Two days ago a new man arrived with her food, allowing her to go to the bathroom on her own and without her blindfold. He made polite conversation with her hesitating in locking her in.

She sat and ate the last piece of bread and cheese and washed it down slowly with a few mouthfuls of water. She curled up in a ball to try and keep warm and eventually fell asleep. She slept fitfully that night, more so than usual, and her dreams were very disturbed.

She awoke to the sounds of the birds outside and traffic off in the distance. The room felt very cold. As her eyes adjusted to the light she had to blink a few times. The door was open and she waited for the man to appear. As the minutes ticked by and no sign or sound of him, Sara carefully, but steadily, made her way to the open door. She peered out and listened. Nothing! Over in the far wall the outside door was open and she made a dash for it.

Her heart pounded in her ears as she ran and was fearful to look back. She ran and ran, eventually her lungs and legs giving up on her. She slumped in a heap. In the distance she heard a noise and as it got closer she mustered up all her energy to stand and wave. It was a big black car and the passenger door opened and the driver spoke "Get in."

Sara was so relieved that she sat in and the driver reached over her and closed the door. She looked behind over her left shoulder making sure she was not being followed as the car pulled off. The noise from the automatic locking system clicking made her feel safe and as she turned her head towards her knight in shining armour, Sara froze!

It was the man from the shed. He turned his head towards her and spoke.

"You are safe. You are in good hands now."

Sara screamed, wriggling in her seat she tried to unbuckle the safety belt but to no avail. The car came to a sudden stop and the engine died. Sara was so scared she was unable to move.

"Sara, please believe me that I am going to help you. My name is Jason, hesitating for a moment, your older brother."

"Older brother" she spluttered.

"It does sound unreal, and if I was in your shoes I too would be very dubious, but please let me explain."

Nodding Sara just stared at him.

"I was ten years old when my father disappeared and following extensive searches by the police and private investigators, he was never found.

In my early twenties I was contacted by a solicitor and to make a long story short, my father was still alive but was terminally ill.

He had become a drug baron and had made many enemies. It was then that I found out that I had a little sister. I did not want any dealings with him as he was living off the proceeds of illegal means."

He continued, "A year ago I started the process of finding you and you had just been found when you were kidnapped. Eventually I found out who had taken you and it took time for me to infiltrate the gang."

"You are safe now," he said, as he started the car and they drove off to safety.

TWO SOLDIERS

Ada Vance

Jim was standing up as he drained the final dregs from the porcelain cup, this would be the last for some time, and from now on it would be tin mugs. Tomorrow he would be back to army cooking and grey rough army blankets. Mother's cooking would be a dream to hold on to.

The few days leave had flown past and he would miss home and being spoiled by his widowed mother Stella, but, looked forward to rejoining his military comrades tomorrow. Jim and twenty fellow officers would be getting on with a six weeks advanced combat training course on Monday.

Thomas, his neighbour, would be on his way by now, they would meet on the bus and travel together to the train station. The plan was to catch the twelve noon train.

Stella helped him into his army great-coat, swept the clothes-brush across the shoulders admiring the epaulet – one squat v that signified his rank as Lance Corporal, she meant to say goodbye at the door but found herself walking alongside him through the garden.

They walked briskly past the flowers, a row of healthy vibrant red cactus dahlias that seemed to stand to attention and nod goodbye in the gentle September breeze.

In the distance the bus chugged along the road and mother and son reached the end of the lane just as it drew to a halt. It was empty. Thomas had said they would travel together but no doubt he would be at the station.

"Off back then" said the driver, "sure you'll be home again in no time at all; they say it will all be over by Christmas."

Stella raised her left hand to pat Jim's cheek and with her right hand like a magician, slipped two coins from her apron pocket and dropped them into his coat pocket. "Good hearty dinners for you and Thomas before you get on that boat" she whispered, "now, a safe journey and write soon."

The long journey would take them first across the country to Dublin, onto the boat to England and then another train journey to the army base. Hopefully there would be no delays, five o'clock tomorrow was the deadline and being late was not an option.

Thomas wasn't at the train station; Jim fidgeted and watched the clock as the minutes ticked away.

He was checking his papers and tickets for the third time when he heard the rumble of the distant train – Thomas was cutting it fine. Jim boarded the train and stood in the doorway, eyes fixed on the station entrance door, the whistle blew and doors slammed shut one after another, Jim jumped down on to the platform just as the train pulled off, there was another train in two hours, it would be cutting things fine but he couldn't go without his comrade.

Jim was worried and annoyed when he boarded the next train alone, Thomas was going to be in big trouble and he knew that only if everything ran on time would he avoid punishment. The journey was slow but he caught the boat. The connecting train in England was delayed and hungry and exhausted he arrived back at training camp just before midnight, seven hours late.

As punishment Jim was stripped of his Lance Corporal rank and sent within 72 hours to the Battle of the Somme. Thomas would be placed on the list of deserters. There was no time for combat training or any preparation much less a chance of writing to his mother.

As Jim waited to board the transport ship, physical fear climbed his spine, he stood gazing at the distant channel, what lay behind it was frightening, he tried not to think about Thomas.

The battalion was ordered to the trenches, foul smelling mud, injured men, moaning and groaning, endless battle noises from gunfire and shelling.

When the sniper bullet hit Jim, the shock took his breath away, a force in his chest and he fell hard on his back into the mud, sounds swirling, his ears ringing, blessed oblivion.

Jim drifted in and out of consciousness as around him people sorted the living from the dead. A gentle hand is stroking his left cheek, the red cross medical sister knows the soldier will not survive the day so he will be put outside the tent in an area where the dying are made as comfortable as possible.

Although exhausted to breaking point the nurse is aware he is conscious. She looks him in the eye and smiles, she knows hers will be the last face he will ever see.

Jim tried to smile back; he gets a glimpse of the red cross and brown wavy hair. Mother and red flowers floated in his thoughts an instant before he became a 'killed in action' war casualty statistic.

On a small plaque in a small church Jim's name is engraved along with six other from the parish. It reads 'IN LOVING MEMORY OF THOSE WHO LAID DOWN THEIR LIVES IN THE GREAT WAR 1914-1918' and it simply ends with.

'GREATER LOVE HATH NO MAN THAN THIS THAT A MAN LAY DOWN HIS LIFE FOR HIS FRIENDS'

Thomas died in 1988. His obituary in the newspaper read: - 'in his ninety first year, predeceased by wife Betty, survived by his six children, fourteen grandchildren and thirty-six great grandchildren.'

BEHIND BARS

Aisling Doonan

The soft tick tock from the mantle clock seemed at odds with time itself. Drawing out each second to its fullest before finally submitting to its loss. Sun beams saw dust motes pirouette in their spotlights on the rectangular tables by the windows. Jem busied himself, unhurriedly, with the polishing cloth on the pint glasses, making satisfactory squeaks as they circled in his large hands. He placed each glass, glittering in the light, behind the bar in readiness for the evening regulars. The bar smelt of old paper with a hint of spice, from whiskey and wood and the constant warmth of the turf fire. The fire was never let out, banked up with soft grey ash after closing time and the embers coaxed from their slumber every morning. It was a matter of pride that the fire never died, the locals were all well used to Jem coddling it like a baby, albeit a cranky colicky one who never slept.

The little brass bell on its curled stem tinkled as the narrow front door opened and Billy and Tom shuffled in. They took several moments to cross the cracked tiled floor to settle themselves in their usual spot by the fire in the easy chairs. The chairs themselves were worn and the stuffing was erupting from its tapestry casing but Billy and Tom had refused to allow Jem to replace them as they were now molded to their particular forms from years of use and were the comfiest seats in the house.

"Well?" Billy threw his finger in the air and gave a sideways nod to the bar.

"Howiya Jem, alright? Any news?"

"No, lads, not a thing, what can I get ye?" Jem adjusted his glasses with the back of his wrist, the stripy red tea towel still in his hand.

"Two pints when you're ready Jem" surprised at his own presumption, Billy turned to Tom and said "It was a pint you wanted, wasn't it?"

"A bike?" Tom squinted incredulously at him "What are you on about, do I look like I'm fit to ride a bike at my age?"

"A pint" Billy barked "You daft eejit, did you forget your hearing aid?"

"No, I don't want lemonade, I'll have a pint thanks" Tom sat back and took the paper off the table to catch up on the racing news.

Billy ambled over to the wooden bar and leant on it with his good elbow. "Come here" he said in a low voice "I hear you had trouble during the week."

Jem took his time, pouring each pint, watching the pale swirls twirl and rise as he righted the glass. "Yep, I did."

"You had a bit of a break-in?" Billy waited patiently; hearsay was one thing, getting the story from the source quite another and he liked to have his facts straight, for when he passed it on again. No one could ever say Billy didn't tell a good story. "Wednesday evening was it?"

"Yes, I was here in the bar, cleaning the glasses as usual. I had the radio on for the news and I was thinking of the nice bit of steak I got in the butchers for tea. Trying to remember if I had any pepper sauce in the press to go with it and wondering was I in a fried onion mood. D'yis know lads, there's no better meal than a juicy medium rare steak, piping hot with a bit of sauce and fried onion. My mouth was beginning to water and I could feel the gurgles in my…"

Billy slapped the counter abruptly "Jaysus Jem, I didn't come here for cookery demo."

"Who's laid low?" Tom chirped, four eyes stared back at him but gave no response.

"So what happened on Wednesday, you know, the theft" Billy waved his hand in a circle to encourage Jem back to the point.

Chuckling, Jem never slowed the gentle momentum he had going between glass and tea towel.

"As I was saying, I was cleaning the glasses. I went into the back there to get the matching tea cups and saucers for the ICA meeting in the snug that evening, you know how the ladies like their matching crockery. Very sensitive to any chips or cracks and heaven forbid if there wasn't a matching sugar bowl and creamer. I have my mother's old set, beautiful it is, delicate porcelain with dainty little yellow flowers on it. Usually I wouldn't let even the parish priest drink out of it for fear of breaking it but I trust those ICA ladies with my…"

Billy smacked the counter again "Jem, please, don't do this to me, this is serious."

"Very serious", Tom parroted from the comfy seat. Momentarily dazed Jem and Billy gawped at him. "Is my pint ready yet?" He shook the newspaper innocently and bent his head back to stare at its pages.

Billy retrieved the pint from the counter and set it in front of his friend and then hurried back for his own.

"Now, as you were saying."

"Yes, the ICA ladies."

"No, no, no, the theft" Billy's eyebrows were furrowed in the exertion to get to the guts of the tale. He took a deep breath and laid both hands flat out in front on the scarred polished wood.

"When I came out of the back room, with the tray of cups, I noticed that some of the chairs were moved and the door out to the back yard was ajar. So I stood for a moment and…"

"Did you not hear the bell of the door?" Billy asked, fully immersed now in the story.

"No, and that puzzled me, because I usually do. Did I ever tell you I have ears like a bat, I hear everything? When I was a boy the other lads at school used to get me to do sentry duty when they snuck down to the kitchens after hours for food. We had some craic in those days; I always got a large share because I never once let them down. I could hear the headmaster's footstep from a mile away, no joke. He used to wear these leather soled shoes that…"

Billy groaned and tapped the counter with his fingers.

"Ah, yes. Anyway, the door was ajar, so I went to investigate. I had only been gone for about ten minutes. I had to gather all the crockery and inspect each piece before I put it on the tray and it takes time to do a good job right. Society's biggest problem today is that nobody takes pride in their work anymore."

Billy glared, Jem paused and nodded.

"I noticed that the shed door was also open. No one was about, I could see inside the shed so I knew there was no one in there. I had a look around and checked each shelf, but nothing was out of place except for my brand new drill bit set. I had seen it on special offer in Halfords only last week and I was delighted as it had every size imaginable and I could use it for almost any job. There were bits for wood, and metal and all sorts. I was so overjoyed, sure didn't I have it in here the day I got it and showed it to all of you?"

"You did, I remember it very clearly, so I do." Billy nodded sagely. "There was a good crowd in here that night. Do you think it was a local who did it, stole your drill bits?"

"Calf nuts? Sure why would you need calf nuts and you not a farmer" Tom frowned over the paper again.

"Drill bits" Billy roared at him. Tom shook his paper again and retreated behind it.

"Well, I had a think about it, and I don't like to cast aspersions on anyone I'm acquainted with, but I have come to the conclusion, and not lightly I might add, that yes I know the culprit."

Scandalized Billy took a step back. "No!"

"Yes. And I'll tell you why. The light fingered pup knew I'd be busy in the back, knew to silence the bell on the door and knew exactly where they were going and what they came to get."

"You're right, you're right" Billy nodded "and did you notify the guards?"

"No, I did not. I think that, as nothing else was taken and I have a fair idea who it was, I will sit and wait."

"Wait for what?" Billy leaned in.

"For the plundering oaf to show himself" Jem brought his wrist to his glasses again and he grinned in self-satisfaction.

"And you know who it is? How?" Billy wracked his brains for a reliable culprit.

"Do you remember Billy, a certain gentleman acquaintance of ours, who is fond of the odd practical joke? A gentleman who once tried to steal my turf so that the fire would starve and the heart of this humble little establishment would stop beating?"

Billy's grin grew with the light of recognition behind his eyes.

"I do, I do. He was there that night you showed us the drill bits, very interested in them wasn't he?" He said slowly, nodding and relaxing.

"So, how do you plan on drawing this young burglar?"

"Oh a burger? No, I'm not hungry yet Billy, thanks, but I'll have another pint" Tom waggled his empty glass in the air.

"Patience Billy, he will come to me, no worries, he will come to me" Jem gently poured another pint and set it on the counter in front of him. He bent momentarily and when he reappeared he had something in his hand.

"Because I stole his drill" Jem grinned.

A STOLEN DAY

Julie Williams

Parking behind the sand dunes Jackie locked her red Mazda, shouldered her rucksack and set out to explore. Her eye had been caught by a bold flash of colour as she had driven along the coastal road and today for Jackie, time was not to be watched or counted. Today, time could be stretched to pause, even to stop for a while.

The brisk sea breeze lifted her hair, she felt invigorated, drunk on good clean fresh air and the excitement of a stolen day.

She walked the tide line, beachcombing for sandy, salty treasures, before heading back up the beach to a rocky outcrop. It was greasy under her bare feet and the strong, pungent aroma of seaweed filled the air as it dried out in the warmth of the day.

Making her way carefully over stones and through rock pools, she spied the vivid splash of colour she had seen from the road. Big plastic weights fixed onto the nets of an upturned fishing boat. They glowed brightly in the sun. For a while she explored, her hands stroking the textures. Soft warm wood, netting sticky with salt, ridges on shells and smooth stones. Her tummy growled, so she sat to eat a simple lunch of sausage rolls and a banana, washed down with a few swigs of lukewarm tea.

She read for a while, then leaned back against the warm hull of the little boat, the rucksack her pillow, the hiss and swish of the tide a gentle lullaby.

Jackie slept.

Layla and Hugo smiled at each other and leaned forward. Almost crouching over Jackie's resting body they watched her sleep for a while, focusing on the rise and fall of each breath. The shadows they cast were stretched long and thin by the angle of the evening sun. Dressed totally in black, they seemed to absorb the brightness of the day; it was only reflected back by the bone whiteness of their faces and hands.

"Hey there Missy." Hugo spoke softly. "Tides a comin' in, time to wake."

Jackie opened her eyes and registered, with some degree of alarm, the sight before her.

Hugo was smiling, a lazy, generous smile, that showed teeth, big solid gnashers, slightly green and not smelling too great either.

"I didn't realise, thanks for waking me" she hesitated at accepting Layla's outstretched hand, which pulled her swiftly to her feet. She managed to stifle the urge to wipe hers clean on the leg of her jeans, but it felt soiled and greasy after the brief contact with Layla's flesh.

Hugo and Layla faced her, their backs to the sun, blocking the heat of the day, making Jackie's skin pucker with goosebumps. She was flustered and anxious to be gone, to reach the safety of her Mazda and be speeding away, back to the normality of her ordinary life.

Scrambling to her feet, Jackie was eager to walk away, but reluctant to show them her back, exposed and vulnerable. Layla reached over and lifted the rucksack. It held Jackie's phone and purse. She sucked in a shaky breath as Hugo moved silently to her left side, linking her arm.

"We will see you to your car. Come Layla." Layla moved up closer and snaked an arm around Jackie's waist.

They made an awkward trio as they headed for the car park. As they neared the Mazda, Jackie wriggled free from Layla's embrace and reached into her jeans pocket for the ignition key, straining against Hugo's cool damp arm, leaning forward to reach the lock as fast as she was able.

Her hair hung limply against her cheeks and neck. Her body was damp with a cold sweat and she was shaking with the relief of sitting safely in the driver's seat. Layla handed her the rucksack and Jackie started the car. Hugo was leaning on the open door, relaxed and still showing those teeth in a semblance of a smile that didn't reach his eyes. They were dark, shiny buttons and Jackie couldn't bear to look into that gaze one moment more.

She tugged the handle and Hugo's elbow slipped, allowing her to fully close the door, with a solid comforting clunk.

Breathing out slowly, Jackie forced a carefree smile onto her face, found first gear and slowly maneuvered the Mazda clear of Hugo and Layla.

Resisting the overwhelming urge to check the rearview mirror, she exited the carpark driving out onto the road that led back to normal, ordinary and safe. The rucksack lay beside her on the passenger seat.

A SMALL LEAK WILL SINK A BIG SHIP

Margaret Maguire

She was a strong woman, who knew where she was going in life.

She was first into the office each morning. Cool blond hair tied in a neat knot. Dark navy suit and white shirt. Her skirt coming just above the knee. She always wore high heels so her legs would look long and slender. She had grey eyes, and a pale complexion, helped by her weekly visits to the beauty salon. She ate sparingly, and did a nightly stint in the gym.

Her personality could best be described as arrogant. She had a way of talking down to people, and her sentences contained commands like, "I want this done now" or "I will not accept this."

When she commanded, everybody jumped.

Miss Sheila Maxwell, company director, had to be obeyed.

She started in the company of Electronic Software after she left college, with a diploma in business. She would have liked a degree, but her brain power was not as good as she led people to believe.

She worked hard at company policy, her image, and company men.

She was three years with the company when she heard that Mr. Dowling, Chairman of the Board was about to retire.

Sheila started to get herself ready to fill his shoes. However she had a serious rival in Donald Gerety. He was longer with the company, and he would use everything at his disposal to get his own way. But Sheila felt that she could overcome most obstacles.

One day she heard the girls in the outer office, discussing their visit to the fortune teller. The next night, Sheila decided that she would go along; after all, it would do no harm to have some knowledge of the future. The girls were more than surprised when Miss Maxwell asked if she could come. Just for the fun, of course, she did not believe in such things

So, on Wednesday night, they all set off to 'Madam Marina'.

She was in the back of a pub down town, and a long queue had formed by the time they arrived. Sheila was very nervous. Maybe she should not have come. However, she could not leave now, those silly girls would think her a coward.

After about an hour's wait it was her turn.

Madam Marina sat at a table, on which a number of candles burned. She had lustrous red hair, smoldering dark eyes, and wore a flowing garment.

She took Sheila's hands in hers and turned them palms upwards. The first words she said were. "Well, you are certainly an ambitious woman, but be careful who you trust. Those you work closely with will foil your ambition..."

Sheila asked for more information but all Madam Marina would say was "You are a lady who will have great disappointment in life if you can't open your eyes to those who are against you."

Sheila left the fortune-tellers in a trance. She told herself it was nonsense, but when she got home she poured herself a stiff drink. And then another.

Next morning she woke up late. She pulled on her clothes, taking no care with her hair and make-up. She arrived into work late, for the first time ever, much to the surprise of other staff members.

This was to become the pattern for the following weeks. She started to suspect everyone. She went home worried each evening. She stopped going to the gym, so put on weight. This worried her so she drank more. She felt tired all the time, and fell behind with her work. She could not talk to anyone, as she suspected everyone. And very soon Sheila

Maxwell was not 'chairman material' anymore.

As the old proverb says 'a small leak will sink a big ship', the fortune-teller had started a small leak in Sheila. And sure enough it sank her.

Madam Marina is alone tonight, except for a young gentleman in a smart business suit, on his way from the office. He pushes the wad of notes towards her, saying "Thank you Marina. You did a good job."

He smiles. "The ship has sunk, the job is mine."

COFFEE & INSOMNIA

Julie Williams

Rush of Darkness.
Swift, relentless, cold.
A black veil of sorrow cloaking the land.
Smothering light, joy, tenderness.
Smoky fingers grasping flower petals.
Brittle, brown decay.
The end of beauty.
Darkness brings along two daughters.
Frost & Mist.
Silver, silent, subtle.
Deadly beauty, without mercy or compassion.
Wait.
Time draws on.
A thin, weak band of promise.
Edges over the horizon.
Darkness Frost & Mist tumble away.
Lost, gone.
Silent screams with no echo.
As daybreak shatters the air.

REVENGE

Lionel Mullally

At 68 years of age, Sherlock Holmes knew he was not a young man. He was already breathless from the walk up the three flights of stairs to the top floor apartment. He paused at the door. He leaned back against the wall to steady his breathing and heart rate. 'If Watson could see him now,' he thought.

John H Watson. His faithful friend and the reason for this mission. It was two years since his passing and Holmes missed him dearly. Natural causes and age had been the official explanation for his death, but Holmes knew better. He knew it had been murder. Revenge from an unseen enemy from their past. Holmes knew it had been murder; he just knew. He had no proof and the facts were against him. He had been unable to substantiate his theory. Until now, that was. The police had tolerated him but they couldn't see what he knew, what he felt. They were sympathetic to him, courteous out of habit. He hated being patronised and sympathy galled him.

"It is easier to know, than for me to explain how I know" he had told them.

Sergeant Lestrade, the son of his now deceased former ally dealt with him quietly and respectfully, but firmly told him that all the evidence and facts indicated that John Watson had, at 72 years of age, passed away in bed due to a recurrence of a dormant fever. Forty years earlier in 1880, Watson had been wounded in the Afghan war and had contracted enteric fever. A type of typhoid fever, it had impacted on his health, and was the cause of him being invalided out of the Army. It was while recovering in London that he met Holmes. His stories of his adventures with the consulting detective had enthralled many, yet at times irked the private Holmes. He did learn to tolerate them and now often reminisced as age led him to look back on and review his past. So, when all was said and done, he owed this much to John. He had to find his killer because he, Holmes, knew, and believed and felt that Watson had been murdered. The facts though, eluded him. Until now.

Word had reached him from an old Baker Street Irregular, weren't they all old now he thought, that John's death had been chemically encouraged. The fever dormant in him had been sparked into life with the injection of a live culture. Holmes' enquiries were then more focused and he embraced all with a passion. He sought out the facts, pursued the leads and would, he was sure, obtain the proof necessary for Lestrade. He wrote to him, explained this in great detail, yet, received no reply or acknowledgement.

Months of whispers, of names and dead ends had led now to this address and to one name. A man from Holmes' past; Sebastian Moran, Colonel, retired and formerly the principal assassin for the late Professor Moriarty. Moran, described once by Holmes as the second most dangerous man in England, had been released from prison the year prior to Watson's death. The facts were accumulating and the theory starting to emerge. Holmes could sense it, he felt it. He knew he was right.

He removed his pocket knife. The engraving, *To Sherlock, our eternal appreciation, Lestrade and The Yard* still clearly shone. He opened it out and used the thin blade to separate the bolt in the lock and opened the door. He entered slowly and stopped. The room was bare, save for a trunk in the centre of the floor. Holmes scanned the room, walked to the internal door and was satisfied that he was alone. He approached the trunk, went on one knee and placing his knife on the ground beside him, opened the trunk. It was empty apart from a nondescript steel bar. Holmes removed it and studied it. It was of generic design and had no distinguishing features. He held it to the light from the window, turning it in his hands but could discern no markings or indentations of any kind. Curious, but his suspicions were aroused. A noise from behind him startled him. He pivoted to look. Moran had entered the room. Their eyes met and Sherlock could feel the heat and hatred emanating from them. Moran had aged. Prison, since his arrest for trying to kill Holmes years earlier, had taken a toll. Though jaundiced and grey now, Moran still possessed what seemed to be a demonic speed and rushed forward to attack Holmes. Homes hit back, punching Moran squarely in the jaw before he managed to knock Holmes to the ground, where he continued kicking him several times in the side and legs and used his cane to rain some blows towards Holmes's head. Then, as suddenly as he had started, he stopped, turned and hurried from the room. Stunned from the ferocity of the sudden attack, Holmes needed a few seconds to gather his wits and lift himself from the floor to stagger after Moran. He followed the stairs, arriving at the bottom flight to see Moran enter a car door and be driven away. His quarry had eluded him. The game was afoot. A rejuvenated Holmes made off. John's murder was to be solved.

Holmes' contacts proved valuable again and had identified a house Moran was using. Holmes had tried to update Lestrade but when he phoned or called to the station he was informed that the Sergeant was busy, in conference or out of the building. His calls were not returned so, exasperated, Holmes wrote and delivered a note personally to the station stating that he believed that Watson had been murdered, that Moran had done it and that he had found Moran and would get him and the proof needed for the murder.

Holmes worked through the night carrying out surveillance on the house and streets where Moran resided. He was close to Northumberland Road in the Westminster District, ironically only yards from the rear entrance to New Scotland Yard. As dawn broke, Holmes spotted Moran shuffling towards the house he had under observation. He was slow, stooped, no longer as intimidating as he had once been years before. Yet Holmes had still touched his tender side where only hours before this man had kicked and hit him. Holmes moved into the shadows and watched as Moran entered the door of the house. He left the key in the lock. 'A lucky break,' thought Holmes. He debated whether to go once more for Lestrade in the hope he would listen now but knew that Lestrade would again demand facts and proof first rather than just theory. He reminded himself of the warning he had given Watson during the encounter with *the* woman, Irene Adler; *that it was a capital mistake to theorise before one has data. That insensibly one begins to twist facts to suit the theory instead of theories to suit facts.* But this was John's murderer. He knew it. So he allowed himself to disregard his own advice. Holmes hurried across the road. He paused at the door, quietly opened it with the key, and entered.

The house had a lived-in feel to it. The warmth of the evening's fire could still be felt. Holmes walked in further. The silence within aroused his suspicion. He moved carefully towards the kitchen area, and froze. Moran lay on the ground. He lay on his back, his head at an angle, his face pulped and a pool of blood gathering about him. To his left was a bloodied iron bar and Holmes's gaze lowered automatically to a knife protruding from Moran's stomach. A bloodied circle grew about the knife in stark contrast to Moran's white shirt. Holmes was shocked. Moran's death rattle could be heard. 'This must have just occurred' he thought. 'But how?'

"Hello Sherlock" came a voice from the rear door.

Holmes looked. A man, neatly dressed, probably in his early forties, slim build, with short dark hair and an aquiline nose had addressed him.

"Who are you? What happened..?" stammered Holmes, indicating Moran.

The other man smiled.

"He was dying anyway. Cancer. He had only days, at most a week to live. We discussed it and his final wish was to gain revenge on his captor. That's you, Sherlock. The Colonel was always loyal to my family, to my father especially. You remember my father, Sherlock? You described him as the Napoleon of crime! You killed him at Reichenbach Falls."

"Moriarty!" Holmes gasped, feeling the blood drain and a pressure build in his chest.

"Indeed, and I am my father's son in so many ways. You almost ruined our business Sherlock. Thankfully, the black market during The Great War sustained and elevated us immeasurably. I watched over Moran while he was in prison, and ensured his family wanted for nothing. He was loyal always and now in this final act, his desire for revenge on you is complete."

"You killed Watson" yelled Holmes, as he slumped against the wall, the pressure in his chest building and his own breathing becoming ragged.

Moriarty laughed.

"No, he did die of natural causes. But when we heard that you refused to accept it we developed a strategy. We fed you suggestions to help you convince yourself that you were right. And it worked! You ignored your own cardinal rule and allowed your theory to twist and to suit the facts as they appeared. You were WRONG Sherlock, wrong!"

"What was it you swore by; *that when you eliminated the impossible, that whatever remains, however improbable, must be the truth.* The obvious truth was that Watson died naturally, yet you ignored that. We couldn't have asked for more."

"But the incident at that room last night?"

"Mere theatrics, Sherlock, to lead you along. A risk I know, but one worth taking. Moran wanted his revenge as did I. He didn't wish to suffer with his illness so what better way to achieve our aim than for a sudden death? One that appeared as murder, committed by no less a person than an obsessed Sherlock Holmes himself."

Holmes found himself beginning to slide down the wall as his legs weakened. Despite himself he had to chuckle, and rasped.

"But how could I murder him, Moriarty?"

"The facts, Holmes! Look at the facts. The facts are the proof and speak volumes. Look at the bar on the ground that was used to smash in his head. Is it not familiar looking? Remember your close inspection of it last evening? So guess whose fingerprints are all over that particular murder weapon. Granted, fingerprint evidence is a new science, but the courts will accept it as corroboration; the knife in his guts, Holmes? Look closer. That particular knife was presented to you personally by Scotland Yard with your very name on it. We removed it from you last night; the letter you left at the station for Lestrade – 'I'll get him myself.' We couldn't have asked for more."

"When you saw Moran enter the house only minutes ago, he was returning from that same station. He was there reporting that you had threatened to kill him last night and showed the officer there the cut to his jaw where you had hit him while threatening him. He told them he believed he had seen you hiding outside the house this morning, lying in wait for him. He asked the police to meet him here to show them and they are already on their way. They may even have seen you enter this house after him, Holmes."

"Yes, I killed Moran, Holmes, as he had requested an end to his pain and as a means to destroy you. But the facts, Holmes, and all the evidence, consolidates the theory that you killed him out of a misguided sense of revenge or derangement. The Police already have the theory that you are obsessed with a murder that did not happen, and obsessed with Colonel Moran. Now these facts sustain that theory. I know your methods, Sherlock. Even the police use them now. And as you once stated with some authority, *there is nothing more deceptive than an obvious fact."*

Holmes slid to the floor as Moriarty left, closing the door behind him. Holmes could see him scale the wall into the house next door. The pressure in his chest mounted and he grimaced in pain. The front door of the house was burst open as policemen entered, Sergeant Lestrade at their centre.

They took in the shocking scene quickly.

"Call a doctor," yelled Lestrade as he felt the weakening pulse on Moran's still warm body.

"That's him Sergeant. That's the man I watched moments ago run in here after Mr. Moran," said one young officer, indicating Holmes.

Lestrade was clutching the note Holmes had left him, the words *Its Moran – I'll get him* clearly visible. He saw the bloodied iron bar on the ground, and then his eyes took in the knife in Moran's body, the knife he himself had seen his father present to Holmes years earlier, the engraving reflecting the light from the room.

He looked across at Holmes.

"My God Sherlock, what have you done?"

The pressure increased in Holmes chest. He clutched it tighter, closed his eyes in pain and all went dark.

DEATH NOTICES

Kevin Patrick

Death Notices calmly read
across the wireless sound.
Of reposing, remains and requiems
in steady tones never loud.

No flowers, House Private
donations can be sent to
Townlands, Addresses,
Wards and Homes of Rest- to- view.

Our Lady of this, Our Lady of that,
some passed away peacefully,
some died so suddenly.
It was a mercy, a blessing,
a sweet release.
It was so unexpected,
so quickly, such disbelief.

For the listeners some greedy
for news all about,
who'll be there? See and be seen,
sympathise then get out.

For others a reminder
of their own dwindling days
or of their loved ones
just passed away.

Or they didn't care much
for that one,
their ways and their clover,
but when all's said and done
we'd better call over.

So the Ritual-Rhythm
of Grieving can start.
Before they walk from the Grave
with the strain in their hearts.

To be thought of, recalled,
reminisced and chewed over
by those who now yearn.

By the mourners
leave takers
the diggers
and worms.

THE FINAL SOLUTION

Aisling Doonan

"Sherlock, Sherlock, can you hear me?" The voice was familiar; I felt pressure on my wrist, two warm dry fingers and a thumb carefully placed. Then silence. A bell sounded and whispering footsteps padded to my right side. More pressure on my wrist, soft and smaller this time, delicate bones and a slender hand.

"I thought his eyes flickered for a moment, false alarm, sorry."

"No change, I'm afraid. His vitals are good, he has angina and suffered a concussion, but he should come to of his own accord" her voice was melodic and oriental; she had to reach up to check my drip, wafting rose water. She let go of my wrist and I drifted and all the comforting noises faded away.

I began to dream, dream of her. How delightfully complicated a creature she was, her intelligence never dimmed and neither did my high opinion of her. Oh Irene, how long have I waited to see you?

"He's smiling, can you see? Look there, you missed it again, he was smiling I tell you" the gentle background hiss of equipment lulled me into a half sleep, I may have spoken aloud. Irene. I hovered, neither awake nor asleep. I felt completely relaxed in body, my mind palace open to me, willing me to wander as I lay there. I found Irene's final letter to me exactly where I had left it and I read it, holding the photo of her to my chest. We had such a short time together, eyeing each other up like pouncing tigers, eager for a tussle. I fondly regret my only missed opportunity, but duty calls. Placing my sentimentality to one side carefully, I replaced her memories back in their casket and drew my shoulders back and tapped my cane. Time to sort out what had just happened and how I reached this particular sticky juncture.

"Yes sergeant, delighted you could pop in, yes, yes, he's fine. Did you catch him?" That rational voice again, slightly scratchy with age, but still succinct and clear.

"Yes, we caught him crossing the bridge; he's in custody now Sir, he wasn't expecting us to be waiting for him, got quite the fright as he sauntered haughtily into our checkpoint." Soft English accent, East End London, Irish mother, I filed the voice away as I smiled again.

"Oh yes, I see Sir, he did, he smiled again! Do you think he can hear us?"

"Yes, I very much think he does, he misses nothing, even when unconscious." He was smiling, I could hear the corners of his mouth rise and his eyes crinkle. A bubble welled up in my chest; it was full of light and liberating. It was healing too and I could feel strength returning to my old bones.

I moved swiftly, cane tapping the ground rhythmically as I carefully chose the next room to walk into. Reichenbach Falls, the final problem. I sent John purposely away to take on Moriarty by myself. I told myself it was to protect him, but I was arrogant and wanted to fix my problem my way. The years afterwards, that I had left John to grieve for me, were a necessary evil. The ends justified the means and I was able to outwit my enemies. Content, I moved on to my next destination.

"His feet are twitching, should you call the nurse again?"

"No, he's fine, I think he's dreaming."

John couldn't resist a good murder in a room that was locked from the inside. I wasn't in the least bit surprised to find him there alone, that late March day. I was disguised as a plain clothed policeman and then as a book seller, when I spoke with him briefly. He looked puzzled but I still laugh when I see the look on his face when I revealed my true self when his back was turned for a moment. What a day! He was rendered speechless, before anger took hold of him. I did what I did because I had to. The details I meticulously planned were all for one ultimate conclusion. The end of Moriarty.

"He's frowning now, getting restless Sir" anxiety had crept into his voice. Chair legs scraped roughly against the linoleum floor and a thigh bumped into my bed. My blood still pumped stubbornly in my veins as a clock ticks and he found my pulse again with a practiced touch. I could feel the tension leave his shoulders in that second of tactility. I was almost ready. I had one last place to visit.

Mary Watson. My chief adversary to John's time and loyalties. I had no time or energy to give to her and by the time I returned from my travels she was gone and John was all mine again. In my delight I didn't register his loss. In my impatience I overlooked one small but critical thing. Family.

I chose not to entertain those whose ties to us are made with blood rather than choice. How those ties can bind you tighter and heighten retribution. How a man's life work can pass from father to son and gain momentum and greater meaning. I can finally admit, I overlooked something and it was a grievous mistake. It was time to open my eyes.

"John?" There was a sudden shuffling of feet and two sets of legs hurried to my side.

"Ring for the nurse, quick, he's waking up" the bell tinkled impatiently and his hand grasped mine.

"Sherlock, are you awake, how are you?"

"John" I croaked again, my throat was dry and the words rasped and cut it.

"Shhh, yes, it's me. I'm here, how did you know?"

I struggled to try and sit up; two pairs of strong hands raised me up on the pillows. My eyes couldn't focus properly; they blinked and squinted for a few moments against the light.

"Reichenbach Falls, you copied the master, you faked your own death to draw Moriarty's son out from the shadows. And you…" I was gathering strength now and I jabbed a withered finger at Sergeant Lestrade "You knew all about it and were following me, a little irritating shadow, like mud stuck to a Sunday shoe."

John smiled and shook his head "I should have known you would use the time you were unconscious to work it all out, you gave us quite a fright you know, we got you straight to the hospital but if we hadn't been right behind you, who knows what would have happened."

"Is he gone John? Is Moriarty in custody?"

"Yes, all tucked up in a cell, he won't be leaving anytime soon."

"John, I forgive you your deception. I also want you to know, that I'm sorry, about Mary. I never understood before this, what she must have meant to you. I'm sorry if I put the cases above your needs."

"It's ok" he grasped my hand "I understood that at the time".

"Now, how are you going to write this one? I'll be damned if you have me, weak and diminished, while my foes dance around me and you do all the work. No one would believe it anyway." I lay back, outwardly gruff, but inwardly relieved.

All was as it should be.

GOODBYE

Julie Williams

The basket had belonged to Jane's mother, a forgotten item pushed under the stairs. Jane had always loved its shape and balance, the covering still as vibrant as the day it was purchased. She packed the items she needed with care and placed the basket in her car. The light was fading, maybe an hour of the day left, enough for her purpose. Turning off the main road she wound down the window, breathing in the smell of a rural evening. Another turn brought her to Gulladoo Lake

Reaching across for the basket she stepped out of the car. At the rocky shore of the lake she laid the basket in the damp grass and settled herself on her 'Thinking Seat,' the largest, flattest stone of the outcrop, still warm from the day's sun. Sighing with pleasure Lizzie slipped off her flip-flops and wriggled her toes in the sun sparkled water. She reached into the basket for the wine and a glass, opened the bottle and poured a hefty measure. Raising her face in salutation to the setting sun she drank deeply, the Merlot staining her lips.

She lifted the glass in a toast, "Here's to you Mum, may the Gods guide you on your journey."

She drank again, then poured the last of the wine into the water as an offering.

The final item in the basket was a small origami boat. She held the little vessel with gentle hands, waded out and lowered it into the water. A soft push set it on its journey across the lake towards the sunset. She remained standing, knee-deep in the cool water, her wet skirt floating around her calves, a breeze touching her bare shoulders. Shading her eyes with both hands, she watched the boat tremble, then sink from sight.

She blew a kiss, waved and turned back towards the bank, to drive home in the darkness.

THE DANCE OFF

Lionel Mullally

Dubs! And her after coming away without her dancing crystals too. Helen was less than impressed. The evening she had organised had gone so well until now.

A night away for her with her Rodeo Girls Line Dancing group from Mohill to Mullingar had been planned for, well, ages. And it *was* her group. She started them, trained and taught them, and she organised this night away. A few glasses of wine to relax and loosen the formalities, a lovely meal and to follow, the rest of the night in the lounge. She had even arranged for the friendly DJ to play some of the music from her iPod Shuffle in order for her girls to show off their steps.

But, then THEY were there. The Dubs. With their 'dis, dat, dese and dose' and raucous cackles of laughter as they danced around a bag that had 'De State of Yer One' printed boldly on it. There were eight of them; dressed in Faber blouses, Jersey Peg trousers that just had to be from 'Littlewoods So Fabulous Plus' range and one, somehow, poured into a Jersey Print Swing Dress. And now they were taking over the dance floor.

It was time for Helen to make her move. She signalled to her girls with a patient smile that she would ask for a request for them on the dance floor. She missed the eyes to heaven from Claire and Noreen as she signalled the DJ that they were ready.

An easy one to start with 'Louisiana Saturday Night.'

'Kick off your shoes and throw them on the floor' sang the deep tones of Mel McDaniel.

"Isn't that great girls," she said "come on now. Let's do a little dance for them."

With the music pounding out the beat and the wine taking effect, some of the Rodeo Girls giggled as they started with the Louisiana Kick.

Then, disaster. A Dublin accent called her friends attention to the music and dancing. They joined them on the floor. Well there was no way she'd be showing them how to dance. Helen threw a narrow smile at her new partner as she joined in the kicks and steps.

They could dance.

"I do love de Line Dancing so I do" said the Swing Dress. "It does be great gas."

Helen had to up the stakes a bit. She knew Shania

was next on the shuffle with 'Any Man of Mine' and guided The Rodeo Girls into the Watermelon Crawl. Heels forward and back, a hip thrust and pivot right. Helen was enjoying it.

"God, I haven't seen the Watermelon in years" said the Swing Dress "it's so quaint."

Helen felt the blood leave her lips to flush her cheeks.

"Form three walls from the chorus girls, with a Canadian Stomp" she instructed her girls in a commanding voice.

She smiled at Swing Dress and the dance shifted up a gear leaving the Dubs behind. They stepped aside to watch. Helen relaxed.

Dolly Parton hit the high notes then with *'Baby I'm Burning.'* The Dubs laughed.

"Tush Push" they yelled together and took centre place.

A leap to the left, right heel forward, back and forward again; hip thrusts forward and then, something Helen couldn't master, a Rock Step forward. The Swing Dress added a cheeky pivot turn as the middle aged Dubliners joined Dolly loudly singing *'hot as a pistol of flaming desire.'*

Helen spotted Margaret talking and laughing with one of the Dubs. Fraternising with the enemy came to mind. She watched while Margaret laughed as the Dub joked about Boorna Coola Boola, as if she was the first to say it ever!

Brooks and Dunn sang from the speakers with '*Boot Scootin Boogie.*' Helen called a four wall dance. She'd show them. The Electric Slide followed by her trade mark CC Scuffle, a Rodeo Kick and Stomp from the girls, to finish.

"That's great," said the Swing Dress, surprising her, "that's the CC shuffle, never seen it done like that before. Great Triple Step too."

Helen relaxed a little.

Johnny singing 'Walk the Line' filled the room then. "Remember Colin Farrell doing dat on de telly?" said one of the Dubs.

"He can walk the Line with me anytime!" answered a Rodeo Girl. They all laughed. 'Cotton Eyed Joe' finished the set.

"Here" said the Swing Dress "we've added a Shorty George Step to the 4 Beat Tag at the start of the chorus. I'll show you!"

"I like it" nodded Helen watching carefully.

As the set ended, the ladies mingled, laughed and talked.

"I'm Debbie" said the Swing Dress. "That was a great idea bringing the music like that. We do the Line Dancing up in Dublin, so we do. You must come up some time. It's great."

"Great night Helen," said Claire and Noreen from the Rodeo Girls, as they returned from the bar and pulled the tables and chairs closer to the Dublin group. The laughing and talking continued.

"I love the dress" Helen remarked.

"Penneys" answered Debbie; "I got it in the sale. Twelve euro! It's grand though. Cheers!"

FAMOUS SEAMUS

Kevin Patrick

after a brief illness
came a sudden stillness
Seamus no more
will stir, outside his own front door
he has slipped away
but his words burrow a little deeper today

on the Six-One News
Sharon Ní Bheoláin never looked,
more beautiful in black
as she pressed contributors for words
we mortals lack

yes, they all came to praise and to bury
his own phrases, all over his head
presidents, poets and people
queuing up for their bit to be said

his passport may have been green
and yet he broke bread with The Queen
but sure what did that matter?
all this magpie chatter.

Then a Professor of Poetry, no less
used that most un-lovely of phrases
'The Island of Ireland'.
Which speaks to me of
Men
who went for a pint
but were body bagged
that same night
or
Women and Children
who went shopping
but ended up in bits.
Dark Days.
When History and Misery chimed.

The poet of the people,
for the people
whatever church
chapel or steeple
you attend
or none.
To him,
for us,
for everyone.

SNOW ANGELS

Margaret Maguire

I could feel them gathering. The dark calmness. The heaviness in the air. The feeling of suppressed excitement.

"It's going to snow" they said in the supermarket. I laughed out loud at their ignorance.

A few people turned to look at me, then quickly turned away, as if they had been caught in a shameful act.

I continued to fill my basket with one of everything.

My married son Paul might call with Cathy and the children. My grandchildren. But they would not stay long. They never did. They had to get back for their jobs and school. They probably would not stay for tea.

They inhabited a world of computers, mobile phones and package holidays. So I filled my basket with one of everything and went home to prepare for the calm quiet which was approaching.

I knew they would soon start arriving, fluttering from the heavens. Their light bodies blowing in the wind. The Snow Angels were coming.

I made tea, then washed up and decided to go for a walk. I put on my red coat. Red, they say, is a positive colour.

Sometimes I see red. But today the red mist has cleared, I feel like me again. I won't wear anything on my head; I want to feel the kiss of the Angels as they land on my head and face.

I walk down the road and then turn left on to the road that leads to the woods. Suddenly I feel a light touch on my face. I look up and there they are, dancing down to the earth, the Snow Angels in all their glory.

I wander on, the trees soon surround me. The angels are coming fast now.

They lie on each branch to rest. Soon there is so many that they form a blanket, lying on top of each other until they cover the green branches.

I am caught up in their dancing joy. I start to dance. It's so long since I danced. I still remember my dancing days in Morrow Hall. It was at a dance there that I met Jack. A tall skinny youth. A fine dancer.

He was the strong silent type, or so I thought. But what I took for strength was in fact weakness. Jack hated responsibility and loved the pub.

I was still myself when our son was born. Still the young, together homemaker full of plans. When Paul was ten years old, Jack started staying out all night. One night he just never returned. The letter requesting a divorce came three months later.

That was the first time that I noticed the Snow Angels. They came to enfold me in a beautiful silent world. Where only I belonged.

Soon after this the battles started. Some people said I must snap out of it. 'Out of what?' I liked where I was.

They took me to the hospital six months later. It appeared that I was spending too much time with the Angels. The time had come for me to leave them behind. I joined the sunshine sometime after that. And sunshine is no place for Snow Angels.

So why was I so excited today when I felt them coming?

Perhaps I was ready to join them again. And so I dance, as I feel the wild joy of a child again. Around and around, arms outstretched. The dance of the Angels. On and on we go twirling together.

It's dark now. I feel so tired. I will sit in a tree, just like the Angels, and rest a while. Perhaps sleep.

The voices echo in the stillness. "She must be here. I saw her come in".

"Hold on, I think I see her". Then the frantic voice of my son calling. "Mum, are you all right?"

"Oh Paul, my son, don't you know? I am with the Angels. They have caressed me with their coldness and covered me with their calm brightness.

I am safe."

VARIATIONS ON A MORNING

Julie Williams

Awaken early.
Dart out of bed.
Crack open the window.
Snuggle and burrow back under the duvet.
Lay still, quiet.
With ears alert for the first notes of.
The Dawn Chorus tuning up.
Watch as light steals through the gap
between the curtains.
And dust motes dance in a ray of hazy sunshine.
Allow toes to wriggle and the mind to wander.
Making mental background checks
for tasks to come.
Ready for the morning cuppa?
Wait, stay lazy with a dry throat.
Dozing, drifting.
Allow the warmth and birdsong to lull you.
Welcome to the start of a brand new day.

Dull mornings require more effort and imagination.
Listen to the rhythm of the raindrops as they
pitter patter on the pane.
These herald the arrival of a damp start to a day.
Do not be mislead make the chilly leap.
Thrust open that window.
Then bury yourself.
With cosy socks and fluffy pyjamas.
Snug as a bug in a rug.
Watch as the Breeze whooshes in
to tickle at the nets and dance with the curtains.
Breathe deeply of that tangy air.
Fill your lungs with its texture.
Maybe a cuppa will be carried to your bedside.
A loving gift to wrap.
Your hands around and inhale the steam.
Welcome to the start of a brand new day.

THE AUTHORS

*To Owen & family
enjoy the Book
Margaret 15/12/16*

Helen Corcoran

Helen lives in an old converted farm house on top of a hill overlooking three counties and three provinces. Six generations of her family have lived there since it was built in the 1860's. Inhabiting history creates a sense of connection between the past and the present.

Stories, written and spoken, have always been an important part of Helen's life, beginning with stories told to her and her siblings by their mother.

Since joining a new creative writing group in the local library four years ago, Helen has enjoyed the journey of sharing her writing with like-minded people. She has had several pieces of writing published in various local books.

Aisling Doonan

Aisling has lived in all four provinces and currently resides in Carrigallen via Cavan via Dublin. She hopes to make it across to the West Coast and retire by the sea, preferably in Achill. She is an avid collector of fountain pens and has a feral attraction to all types of stationery. She has been writing stories and poems since she could hold a pen, and took first place in the short story section of 'The Leitrim Guardian 2016' with her story 'I am the Secret Keeper.' She is also a knitted lace enthusiast, taker of many photos and sometimes designer.

Margaret Maguire

Poetry and short story writer and winner of the Dún na Rí literary award 2012. Margaret has also had her plays featured on local radio and performed in the Ramor Theatre and Gonzo Theatre (2008/2009). She joined Scríobh in 2012.

Lionel Mullally

Lionel Mullally is an award winning writer and poet and has been involved in the Scríobh Writing Group since its inception. He has been writing for many years and has been published at home and abroad in periodicals, magazines, local newspapers and on the Internet.

Married, he resides in Arva, Co. Cavan with the woman who made all his dreams come true, and their three children.

By vocation a member of An Garda Síochána he is also a 'Star Wars' fan and firmly believes that delinquents and 'Kylo Ren' can be helped to achieve social maturity by the proper application of 'The Force'.

Kevin Patrick

After many years of phrases, rhymes, rhythms and words walking into his head then departing, Kevin Patrick decided to pick up a pen and paper on his lunchbreak and write some of this stuff down and found that after all, (to his surprise) he had the calling of a poet.

You can hear some more of his original pieces on 'soundcloud.com' along with his songs, if you like.

His favourite biscuit is the design classic, the Custard Cream and Kevin has written an Ode to the same which he hopes will make it into Volume II.

Ada Vance

Ada lives near a rural village in a place where three counties and three provinces meet.

She divides her time between gardening, crafts, cookery and travel.

Meeting so many ordinary people who do extraordinary things motivated her to write, she has pieces published in three recent ICA publications.

Ada is new to the Scríobh group.

Julie Williams

Julie Williams lives in rural Ireland surrounded by small hills known as Drumlins, lots of lakes and beautiful scenery. She has a small dog called Billy, a medium sized Husband and a tiny Mammy. Her passions are photography and playing the ukulele.

Writing is her latest project and Julie is discovering the pleasure of creating poetry and prose.

WRITING IN THE ROUND

Scríobh: Carrigallen Creative Writing Group

Writing is often considered to be a solitary and lonely vocation. The Poet in his Garrett, the Writer in the spare room typing out a novel or manuscript. Or perhaps a busy parent poring over the laptop in quiet concentration when the kids are gone to bed. Solitary writing can be good, but not all the time.

A creative writing group allows writers to share stories, poems and pieces in company along with the social benefits of establishing new friendships and sharing in the synergy and humour that comes from a love of creativity and writing with others.

The following piece is an example of writing together. It was written by ourselves in an exercise called 'Writing In The Round' and begins with a 'trigger' or prompt, which could be an object, a quotation, a piece of writing or indeed anything, that one of the group has brought in.

The trigger is revealed and we simply begin to write a story, inspired by this for a few moments, until the facilitator commands us to finish the sentence we're writing.

Then each person passes their book to the next writer along, whilst receiving a book from the writer beside them.

Crucially each person is only allowed to read the last completed sentence from the book just received before immediately continuing with the 'story' until the next changeover a few minutes later and so on. This continues until their book has gone round the group, back to themselves and the writing stops.

We then have a complete story, or at least seven or eight versions of a story all starting at a similar point but finishing differently. One story is then read out in all its newly written glory and each writer can hear their 'bit' in the narrative. As well as being a lot of fun, the piece usually meanders from one style, pace, tone and plot to another quite rapidly, yet it is a good exercise in thinking fast and improvising.

So consider the following piece a 'Bonus Track' being an example of us all writing together, a collective effort mirroring this collection. The trigger in this case is a 'Monet' painting of a garden scene with two figures.

Indeed the cover of this book is a snapshot of all the different styles of handwriting taken from such a session where our creativity was pooled. But do bear in mind this is an 'unpolished piece' that has been copied down as it was written without any review or proofing. So enjoy the silliness and the humour to finish our first collection and remember, *'a writer is someone who writes'*.

To friendship.

JARDIN DUO

Scríobh: Carrigallen Creative Writing Group

Niamh decided she needed a colour scheme for the garden. Derek suggested flowers and Niamh gave him 'the look' before explaining patiently, again, that her interests, vitality, patience, exuberance, in short her *joie de vivre* had to be explicitly expressed and reflected in the correct colour scheme in the garden.

Derek found himself humming 'flowers are red young man and green leaves are green.'

Any moment now and Derek would surely find himself veering into Dr. Seuss territory. 'Look what spawning children did' he thought. It was either that or dealing with Niamh on the rampage that led to the Swiss Cheese currently replacing his brain!

Colour schemes were the Devil's work, along with the M1 and daytime television.

But old habits die hard. Daytime television could wait, but the order and regularity of the plants and shrubs made her skin itch. Her foot knocked against metal. It was a vicious garden tool lying in the grass. She picked up the rake and began to pull it through the sand. This wasn't relaxing at all!

"Bloody hippies" she muttered, as she drew funny little lines in the sand.

"How on Earth can this be relaxing?" she thought as she focused on making a straight line parallel to the edge of the little sandbox.

"Can't see why the doctor wouldn't just give me some tablets instead of this palaver. The Judge told me I was a danger to society."

"A danger? Me??? I am a greater danger to myself. This OCD is killing me. Imagine having to take my clothes off every time a car horn blows. I was in the middle of Main Street the last time when the Guard came along."

He stood in front of her and she bumped right into him because she was trying to locate her ringing phone from the bottom of her oversized shoulder bag and was not watching where she was going.

"Excuse me," she said meekly, "I didn't see you there."

The man turned around and went to speak, then stopped and smiled a warm, genuine smile. He had kind shining eyes, a lovely smile, was tall and had luxuriant dark hair.

'Oh boy, he's gorgeous' she thought to herself.

He took her hand in his and holding it, held her gaze. Time melted, music played; there was only them in the whole world.

Then, she loudly farted...

He followed with a louder, longer one, smiled lovingly into her eyes and said,

"Atta girl, we'll get on fine you and me."

And they did a satisfying duet.

Putting an arm around her shoulder, they looked for the call for an encore. None came from the silent group, though their mouths were open. So he turned to her and said

"Again?"

She nodded eyes. 'Islands in the Stream' rocked!

SCRÍOBH SCRIBBLES

Thank **YOU** for reading.

Made in the USA
Charleston, SC
12 November 2016